Emily's Stitches:

The Confessions of Thomas Calloway

And Other Stories

By Leverett Butts

Jessica,
Keep Writing!
- LB

Beholden Books
Atlanta, GA
beholdenbooks@ymail.com

For Tina

Eyeballs to entrails, my sweet

Table of Contents

Foreword and Acknowledgements   5

PROLOGUE   11

I. BLINDNESS AND THE FALL   14

II. THE FENCE 'TWIXT HEAVEN AND HELL   23

III. HELL'S DITCH   40

IV. THE DEAD BURY THEIR DEAD IN THE HOUSE ON TOP OF THE WORLD   56

INTERLUDE   74

V. THE PRIMROSE PATH   76

VI. HOME I'LL NEVER BE   97

VII. GETHSEMANE   116

EPILOGUE   129

Poems & Other Stories   131

FIT   133

ICARUS FELL   134

REQUIEM   141

HAND-ME-DOWN BOY   146

LOVE EVER YEARNS   148

NEGATIVE SPACE   151

SERMON   166

GODS FOR SALE, CHEAP   171

MISDIRECTION   176

CHALLENGE   194

Foreword and Acknowledgements

These stories (and three poems) have been sitting around on my hard drive mostly unused since the mid 1990's and the early 2000's. When I was working on my Master's degree at University of West Georgia, I began *Emily's Stitches* as a writing exercise. I wanted to write an entire novel made up of self-contained short stories. When I first wrote it, I thought it had Pulitzer written all over it. When I recently dug it out for the first time in over a decade, I realized I may have overvalued it a bit. While not prize-winning material after all, it is still, however, an enjoyable story. It may not be the great American novel I thought it in my cocky mid-twenties, but it is, I think, a pretty good novella.

The other pieces in this collection I wrote sporadically. The poems (the only poems I've ever written that I felt half-way good about) were written a few months after the last *Emily's Stitches* story when I was recently divorced and teaching high school English at Haralson County High School in Tallapoosa, Georgia. I would like to dedicate them to my old students (who were, by and large, better behaved than Jesus' disciples in "Sermon").

"Requiem" began as another writing exercise. This time the exercise was two-fold: I wanted to turn an actual event in my life into a coherent narrative and I want to tell a story in complete dialogue without an external narrator. When I decided to include it in this collection, I realized I should probably change the characters' names since they were real people. One of my old high school friends, Scott Thompson, had recently published his own first novel, *Young Men Shall See* (available at amazon.com as well as your local bookstore), and I realized that the story I had written years ago would, with only a couple of minor tweaks, dovetail nicely into the world of his novel. I'd like to thank Scott for giving me permission to use his character names and allowing me to dip my toes in his world of River Falls, Georgia. If you have not read Scott's book yet, I suggest reading it before you read "Requiem" as my story takes place a few years after and has direct bearing on one of the storylines in Scott's book.

"Gods for Sale, Cheap" was written only a few years ago for an open-mic reading at the Annual Robert Penn Warren Conference held in Bowling Green, Kentucky. It's another story told completely in conversation (this time a telephone conversation) in an attempt to improve my dialogue skills. It and "Misdirection" are attempts to blend fantastic or mythical elements overtly into the real world and are clearly inspired by writers such as Neil Gaiman and Charles Stross. They are also my favorite two stories in this collection.

Several of these stories and poems have seen print before: "Blindness and the Fall," "Hell's Ditch," "The Primrose Path," "Icarus Fell," "Fit," and "Sermon" were all published in *Eclectic* between 1997 and 2001. "Negative Space" was published in the 2004 edition of *The Georgia State University Review*. "Love Ever Yearns," the most recent story in this new edition, was published in the November/December 2013 issue of *Newnan Coweta Magazine*.

Finally, I would like to thank author Richard Monaco for instigating my first step in self-publishing. I decided to go ahead and publish these pieces in an attempt to understand the formatting requirements for Amazon's Kindle so that I could assist him in getting the electronic edition of his latest book, *Lost Years: The Quest for Avalon*, available for Amazon's Kindle. If you are unfamiliar with Monaco's work, you need to check out his *Parsival* series. It is very much one of the best Arthurian

6

series I have ever read, so good, in fact, that two of the books, his first and third novels, actually were Pulitzer finalists.

Emily's Stitches: The Confessions of Thomas Calloway

Prologue

The first thing you have to understand about me is that I try to keep to myself as much as possible. I go to work each morning, do my job, and go home. I work at the high school as a janitor, so I spend my days cleaning up other people's messes. The last thing I want to do, then, is spend my evenings making my own messes to clean up. I don't own a car because I got no reason to. I live walking distance from both the school and the grocery store. I couldn't afford one anyway without having to go to the bank and borrow money, and while I've no doubt they'd loan it to me, I've never felt right about being beholden to anyone, and I haven't been beholden since high school.

That's the next thing you need to know, I won't be beholden to nobody anymore. That hasn't ever done a thing but get me into trouble, and I've had enough trouble to last a lifetime. I live in the same house I was born in because it was mine. I live there alone because I ain't never been good at sharing my life with anybody else. I just get hurt in the end. Or they do.

I came home from work yesterday evening about five or six just like every other day the last thirteen years. I changed into some jeans and a T-shirt and put on my slippers. Then I got a beer out of the fridge and went on the porch. I like to sit on my porch and drink beer because I can watch the world go by and still feel like I'm a part of it, even if it is a spectator's part. I guess I'd been out there about ten or fifteen minutes when the phone rang. I didn't bother to get up; most likely a wrong number or telemarketer since just about everybody I knew and had any interest in keeping up with had moved away years ago. Let the machine get it and I'd erase the message later.

After another beer, I went back in the house. It was getting dark, and I was getting hungry. I turned on the TV on my way into the kitchen and let the local news play in the background while I pre-heated the oven and tried to decide on the chicken with stuffing and peach cobbler or the Salisbury steak, whipped potatoes, and cherry pie.

"In other news," the TV informed me, "hospitals and banks across the nation, tonight, are trying desperately to upgrade their computerized systems to be Y2K compliant before the January first deadlines. Officials seemed optimistic."

I had steak for lunch, so I decided on the chicken. Besides, the peach cobbler is better than the cherry pie any day. I wish it didn't take so damned long for the oven to heat up. I'd use the microwave, but it hasn't worked in months, and I haven't been able to save up enough money all at once for a new one.

"The Middle East peace talks hit a snag this afternoon when..."

I pulled a soda out of the fridge and poured it into a plastic Dixie cup. I topped it off with Southern comfort, but there wasn't no room for ice. I returned to living room.

"Investigations into Egypt Air Flight 990 continue with few new developments."

I flopped into the easy chair and my drink sloshed onto my shirt. I sucked the spill out and sipped some more from the cup. I glanced over at the phone machine, and the light was blinking, so I pressed the button.

It took me a little to place the voice. Phones always distort voices and this voice had deepened considerably since I last heard it.

"Don't worry, boy," it said, "I'll take care of everything."

"Things seemed peaceful in the small town of Owen, Georgia, today as the men of Strickland Drainage began to empty Lake Harall on the outskirts of town. However, what began as a routine procedure soon turned gruesome."

I turned to the TV screen as the mention of the lake made my stomach sink. The plump, bearded face of Chuck Strickland was staring at me through the camera.

"Well," he said, "we're supposed to drain this 'ere lake 'cause they're gonna build a shoppin' mall out here. It didn't take no time a'tall on account of it wasn't much of a lake to begin with, just a deep pond, really."

The voice of the reporter then began to explain as scenes of an old canvas sack being pushed on a stretcher into an ambulance and of a sheriff's deputy walking around in the mud looking important paraded across my screen.

"This canvas bag was found half buried in the silt of the lake floor. When the workmen investigated their find, they discovered what appear to be human remains inside. The Catagua County Sheriff's Department was called in and they quickly cordoned off the area. The sheriff had this to say:

The Sheriff appeared on the screen, and he, too, looked straight at me when he talked. "Well, we've obviously got a murder on our hands. I mean the body didn't zip itself up in that bag. I reckon it's my job to bring the murderer, if he can be found, to justice. I aim to do just that. Don't worry," his gaze seemed to grow harder, "I'll take care of everything."

I turned off the TV, threw back the rest of my drink, and got up. I put my dinner back in the freezer and turned off the oven. Then I picked up the phone and called a cab.

"Bobby? Yeah it's me. You, too." I hate small talk. "Listen I need a cab over here to take me to Atlanta. How much is that gonna be? No, I got the money, I don't need a tab. When can he get here? A'right, I'll be waiting."

I got here about an hour and a half later, and the desk clerk looked at me all weird.

"Can I help you?"

"I won't be beholden to nobody," I replied. "I did it, and I aim to pay for it."

I. Blindness and the Fall

If you walked through the woods, keeping the creek on your left and went straight 'til you saw the lightning tree what's half dead and bore right, following the foot trail a piece, you'd see my place. Now I didn't live there or nothing, but it was mine just the same. It's where I'd go when I wanted to think about things or just be alone for a while. What it was was an old slave shack from back in the Civil War days, but hadn't nobody lived there in years. Oh, I suppose the occasional hobo'd stop there for a night or two, but I'd never seen one. My daddy told me to stay away from it on account of its being so old and run down. I reckoned he thought it was liable to fall right on my head if I so much as looked at it cross-eyed. But I figured it was safe enough, so I tended to disregard Daddy's wariness and fears and such. Hell, by the time he found out about the place, I'd staked my claim on it about three months.

Anyway that was my place. Now I wasn't but about sixteen or seventeen at the time. But I knew what was what. I figured anything I didn't know after sixteen years of life probably wasn't much worth knowing.

Well, almost anything.

I made an exception for sex. The way I reckoned was, though I didn't know anything at all about the art of conjugal bliss, since people made such a fuss about it, it was bound to be important. So important, I didn't dare let on I was ignorant about it. Well, I mean, I knew the basics. I knew for damn sure that babies didn't come from a stork or under a mushroom or in a cabbage patch. I'd taken health class in school, and Daddy had signed the permission slip for when they divided up the boys and the girls and taken each group off to different areas of the school for "Hygiene Day."

The football coach, Coach Buford, took the boys to the locker room of the gym. Now Coach Buford was a big butterball of a man, and he sweated a lot. I wasn't sure what this talk was going to be about, but I didn't think the locker room was the best place to discuss hygiene, and I sure as hell didn't think that sweaty old Coach Buford was the best authority to be preaching to about it. But that was the way it was going to be, and at least it got me out of an algebra test I hadn't really studied for.

"Alright boys," Buford belched. "You all know why we're here. I'm supposed to talk to you about sex."

Now that got everybody's attention. All the whispering, giggling, and chattering stopped, and we all looked at the coach intently. Now, I didn't think Coach Buford could be any better spokesperson on sex than he could on personal hygiene. It was kind of like a fish reflecting on the dangers of air pollution: not unbelievable exactly, but not all that likely either. One thing I did know about sex was that it required a girl's consent, and the coach, as persuasive as he may have been in the locker room of the losing team at half-time, just didn't seem likely to be able to sway a girl's affections no matter how many showers he took.

He stood there in front of us for the longest time not saying anything but "Well...ah...you see..." and finally "Aw hell, I don't know why they stick me with this crummy detail every spring. Look here boys. If you ain't careful you'll wind up with something Ajax won't take off, and you'll go blind besides. And if I catch you doing it, I'll kick your little perverted asses. Understand?"

We all said yes we did, and since we still had about half an hour, Buford let us practice our free throws on the basketball court.

It was Brother Robert, our pastor at church, who expanded on the dangers of sex for us. He said it was a sin, unless you were married (and then you could only do it one way). It was what caused the Fall of Man (I asked him once about the apple. "Allegory, son, allegory," was all he'd say). It was a filthy, dirty act steeped in putrefaction, and if you did it, you'd suffer eighty different ways of damnation.

After all this hoopla, I knew I'd want to try it. Besides, nothing could be as nasty as all that, unless you did it with livestock or Bertha Crumb, the 350 pound barmaid who apparently charged twenty bucks a pop to do it. But I'd rather guess about it the rest of my life before I'd pay even eighty cents to find out about it from Bertha. I figured if I'm gonna suffer as much as Buford and Robert said, I might as well sin with someone who, if not good looking, at least was halfway agreeable company.

So, sitting on the porch of my place, I'd generally fall to speculating about sex. The only person I'd admit my lack of experience to was Gardener Smith. I knew him from when he was State wrestling champ two years ago. I had just got my job cleaning the gym, and he'd always be practicing with somebody in the afternoons while I cleaned. He was nineteen, so he could offer me the voice of maturity I so desperately needed during this trying time of my innocence.

"Look," he'd tell me. "There ain't nothing to it. All you got to do is be nice to a girl, and she'll let you do it no problem. If that don't work, give her some beer, and she'll come around."

"You done it?" I'd ask.

"Well, now. I don't reckon I should say yay or nay. A gentleman ain't supposed to talk about who he has or hasn't done it with."

"Well, Jesus, Gardener. I didn't ask for their names and addresses. I just want to know if you've done it or not."

Gardener would look off into the woods, take a sip from his beer, and reply, "And I'm telling you it ain't none of your business." (Which I took to mean "I ain't had twenty bucks all at one time yet.")

Gardener tried harder to get me laid than he did himself. Once, he tried to fix me up with Jenny Calhoun, a girl so desperate for love she dated a married man, from Ohio even, for six months until his wife found out and took a potshot at her in the parking lot of Molly's Motel out on Highway 19.

Jenny said I was too immature; I didn't even get to second base.

After this he set me up with Ol' Lady Simms, who was neither. Ol' Lady Simms was thirty-three, divorced, and gossip had it that she was quite the Mrs. Robinson. The year before she had, apparently, extended her personal "compliments" to half the graduating class of Owen High. Rumors aside, she didn't so much remind me of Mrs. Robinson as she did of June Cleaver.

I barely got to first.

Gardener, then, set me up with Anne Marie Harris. Anne Marie was famed throughout the school for being willing to do it with just about anybody. She supposedly did it with a whole football team during half-time of the homecoming game. The visiting team. So Gardener was pretty sure I'd have no trouble.

I never even got up to bat.

After this, he quit trying.

"Either you get up some money or you might as well take your vows, buddy," he said.

About six months after failing to score with Anne Marie, I met Emily.

I had pretty much given up on being able to get lucky with my own personal charms and was just about to swallow my pride and raise twenty dollars, when she showed up. Literally on my doorstep. When I walked into the shack one afternoon, I found her asleep on the floor of my front room. Of course, I didn't realize she was a girl at the time. I figured her for one of the occasional hobos I never saw spending nights in my place. She was all covered up with tattered blankets, scraps of paper, and old clothes. In fact, I couldn't figure out if she was a hobo or the nest of some hellacious rat king like in that Christmas movie with the Russian ballerina fella.

I was just about to sweep her up when she moved, and I found out she was a person. When she sat up, I saw that she was a girl. Not a woman or a lady, a girl. But a very well developed one, if a little filthy.

Emily Blanchard was fourteen, though you couldn't tell by

either sight or sound.

"Who the hell're you?" She growled when she saw me. "And where the hell'd you come from?"

"Well, Missy," I replied adopting my best high and mighty tone, "I might just ask you the same question. This is my place you're messing up."

"Well, if I'm messin' the place up, looks to me like I've had a little help." She looked around the room, staring pointedly at the shot-out windows, punched-in walls, and piles of wood, paper, and leaves in the corners, and snorted.

Then she smiled, and if I hadn't seen her before this, I swear I'd have thought she was twenty-two. This girl was gorgeous.

"You want a smoke?" She began digging into her pile of rags, which turned out to be a cloth sack, and pulled out a couple of cigars.

"Ain't you a little young to be smoking them things?"

"I reckon I'm old enough to do a bunch of things you don't wanna know about."

"That so?" I reached over and took one of the cigars, not wanting to be outdone by this girl.

She didn't answer; she just handed me a scratched up gold Zippo with "J.B." engraved on it. I looked at the letters.

"Joanne?"

"Jimmy. Jimmy Blanchard. My asshole pervert of a father."

"You're Jim Blanchard's daughter?"

"Well, I just said he was my father, and I obviously ain't his son."

Jim Blanchard was a drunk widower who lived off behind the old corn mill on Blevins Road. Gardener said old Jim had killed his wife in a fit of drunken jealousy. I wasn't too sure I believed him, but I didn't discount it outright.

"You still ain't told me what you're doin' on my place."

"I don't think it's really any concern of yours if you wanna know God's truth."

"Well, Missy," I liked using that word "missy;" it made me feel in control. "I don't think I can let you stay here if you don't level with me. Especially now I know where you come from. I'd just soon go tell your daddy where you are, and let him deal with it."

"My name is Emily, and if you so much as breathe at my father, I swear to God and Moses I'll kill you."

I let the matter drop. The place was in pretty poor shape, I figured. Emily wasn't hurtin' nobody sleeping out here, so I told her she could stay as long as she wanted, providing she kept the place up and didn't burn it down. Besides, Old Jim had about a hundred kids, and I didn't think there was any danger of his ever being sober enough to notice her gone until she was at least thirty.

"You mean to tell me you've had a girl stashed up here for a month now and you ain't tried to do nothing with her?" Gardener hadn't been out to my place for a while. His folks gave him a raise on his weekly allowance, and he'd had better places to spend it. He only showed up this Saturday because Bertha had taken a few days off to go visit her mother and help pay for the old lady's electrolysis. When he saw Emily there, he was surprised, but figured I'd kept the secret to myself in order to get in some good experience without having to share. You should've seen his jaw drop when I told him I hadn't even tried nothing with her. I bet a whole herd of sheep could've fit right between his teeth.

"What in God's good grace is wrong with you boy?" He stammered. "You afflicted or what?"

"No. I just hadn't thought much about it, that's all. I mean she's only fourteen."

"I don't rightly see your point. She's a Blanchard; I'm sure she knows all about it. Besides, even if she were a Rockerfeller, I think an exception could be made for a fourteen-year-old looking that good."

"Gardener," I said, feeling a funny sinking in my stomach. "Ain't you got any morals or common decency at all?"

"Sure. I go to church." That wasn't what I had asked him, so

I just turned around and went home.

I thought a good deal about what Gardener said the rest of
that day. Especially about the fact that she was a Blanchard and
probably knew all about it. I thought about Emily not ever
telling me why she ran away, and I thought about poor old
drunk Jim Blanchard and how he'd been widowed damn near
fourteen years. I thought about morality and how Gardener
apparently figured going to church was enough. I wondered if it
was, but I didn't think so. Besides, Gardener only went to try
and see up Sister Joyce's skirts when she sat up so high playing
the organ

That night I had a dream. At first it was like any dream I
might have had whenever I felt particularly frustrated. Only
this time instead of Anne Marie or even Ol' Lady Simms, It was
Emily Blanchard. As soon as I realized it, I got that same funny
sinking feeling in my stomach, and I knew it wasn't no ordinary
sex dream. I was falling from a great height and I couldn't stop.
I couldn't stop. When I did stop, I looked in a mirror, and I saw
Emily under me, but she was tied up and she had a bruise on
her eye. But that wasn't the most disturbing part of the dream.
When I looked at myself in the mirror, I looked like old Jim
Blanchard. But that wasn't the most disturbing part of the
dream. Emily looked into the mirror, too. She said, "Momma."
That was the most disturbing part of the dream. I made myself
wake up.

It was three in the morning, and I couldn't get back to sleep.
I felt dirty, but a shower didn't help me any. I felt ashamed of
myself, even though I hadn't really done anything. I knew why
Emily ran away, and I knew why she wouldn't ever talk about
it. I also knew she could stay at my place as long as she wanted
and I'd never try anything. Not if she lived there until she was
thirty-three.

Three weeks later, Coach Buford was arrested for doing it

with Anne Marie Harris. I guess he heard about her and the visiting team at the homecoming and thought the home team deserved a chance. Anyway, I felt sorry for Anne Marie; I figured she must have had some problems to do it with such a sweaty butterball of a man like Buford. I didn't know what I felt for the coach, confusion I guess. I couldn't think straight. I was in the gym when they came for him and I heard what they got him for. When they cuffed him and took him out, he looked right at me and asked if I'd lock up the office. As they led him away, I called after him. They stopped, and he looked at me expectantly.

All I could think to say was "What about Ajax?" I didn't mean any disrespect, really. But I think he took it as such. He just glared at me as they hauled him out.

I went to the shack that afternoon. I figured Gardener would be there, and I wanted to tell him what happened, but as I neared the place, I realized that everything was real quiet. It was eerie. Then I heard some shuffling coming from one of the shot-out windows, and when I looked, I saw that Gardener was there. All hundred and sixty pounds of him. Emily was there, too.

It was just like my dream, only this time I was the mirror. And this time the sinking feeling was rising. I stood transfixed outside that window, my mind a sheet of white. Gardener looked up at me and grinned. I was stuck floating in my stomach rising towards the white in my head. I couldn't do anything until Emily looked, too. She wasn't crying; she wasn't whimpering; she was just there. She said, "Momma."

To this day, I'm not sure how I got through that window so fast. I only know that it took me about three seconds to reach Gardener. He was still grinning like an idiot when I kicked him in the ribs and knocked him over. He was still grinning like an idiot when I straddled his chest and punched him twice in the nose. He was still grinning like an idiot when he flipped me over and grabbed my neck. Neither one of us saw Emily with the two-by-four. She hit him once to knock him off me, and then he took off out the window.

After he had been gone awhile, I sat up and rubbed my neck. Emily was sitting in the corner hugging her knees up to her chin. She rocked back and forth, but I couldn't tell if she was crying. Maybe.

I took her out to the creek later and watched while she bathed. She didn't look twenty-two anymore; she looked twelve.

"She's just a child," I thought. Then I thought about Ajax and blindness and eighty ways of damnation. I thought about Anne Marie and how she had done it with the coach and the football team. I thought about Jenny Calhoun and the husband from Ohio. I thought about Mrs. Simms and how she was all alone because her husband ran off with his accountant. I even thought of Bertha and her mother's electrolysis. I figured that maybe they all had reasons for what they did, maybe good ones. Just because they had sex didn't make them less people. I realized that nothing, not sex, not anything, could ever be as black and white as Coach Buford and Brother Robert, and even Gardener, made it out to be.

Emily could stay at my place as long as she wanted and I'd never try anything. Not if she lived there until she was thirty-three.

II. The Fence 'Twixt Heaven and Hell

Miss Ruby O'Neal was about eight days older than God. She lived out past the mill village on Coleman Street. Her house, an old shotgun shack, overlooked the unpaved street from a bluff of eroded scrub and red clay. She lived alone except for about a billion cats she kept around, supposedly to eat the rats and snakes she had convinced herself lived under her sofa. Miss Ruby'd lived there for the past seventy-five years, and nobody knew precisely why. When she was much younger, her family had lived up on Montague Street in one of those huge houses with a wrap-around porch and damn near twenty floors. The O'Neal's had been one of the first families in Owen. They had made their money originally from cotton, but after 1865, there wasn't enough help left on the old homeplace to make it a reliable source of income. So in 1885 (shortly after marriage) Ruby's father moved to town, opened the O'Neal Unreconstructed Cotton and Textile Mill, and within three years, had made back all the money the family had lost during the war. Ruby was the oldest of three sisters and the only one left by the time her great-nephew, Parry Beaumont, introduced me to her during the spring break of my senior year in high school.

Parry was the grandson of the youngest O'Neal daughter, Beatrice. Beatrice died when Parry's father was born, and since her husband had run off with the daughter of a mill hand, there wasn't nobody to raise Mr. Beaumont, so Ruby took him in and brought him up.

"That old lady's been crazy for damn near eighty years," Parry told me and Gardener once. "Just ask anybody. She used to make my daddy sleep in the attic because her fiancé was sleeping in the guest room."

"Well, now, that *is* strange," Gardener agreed, "but I don't think that's necessarily crazy. You would think the fiancé'd be sleeping in Ruby's room,"

"No, she was crazy," Parry insisted. "The fiancé'd been dead over sixty years."

"Oh, now, that's just disgusting," I joined in. "How could anybody live with a dead man for sixty years? What about the smell?"

"My mother's lived with a dead man for the last ten years," Gardener argued. "She never complains about his smell."

"Why don't y'all try not being idiots, just once before you die? Of course she didn't have the man's body in the room. That's just what I'm saying. There wasn't nobody in the room at all, but she still made my daddy sleep in the attic. When he tried to explain to her that the fiancé was dead, she just looked at him and said, 'Well, sir, that's as may be, but he still needs a place to sleep.'"

The first time Parry brought us to meet Miss Ruby, we were on our way up to the mountains to go camping. We stopped by Ruby's house to drop off some vegetables Mrs. Beaumont had set out for her. We found her doubled over in front of her porch. She looked like she was having a seizure of some sort. Her whole body was hunched over close to the ground and bouncing up and down, and she held her left arm out in front of her, apparently unable to move. Her right arm, though, was swinging uncontrollably.

"Damn," Gardener exclaimed. "Looks like the old fruit's gonna keel over dead before we even get a chance to have any fun."

I glared at him, but Parry paid no attention. "What the hell's she doing?" he muttered. "I hope she ain't forgotten her medication again."

As we neared her, Parry began to realize what she was doing. "Oh my Christ." he sighed. "She's got another snake."

And sure enough, we could see that the ol' lady was pulling what looked like a long green rope out of the ground with one hand and swinging a hatchet at it with the other. She finally succeeded in chopping the snake half in two when we walked up behind her.

"Looky here boy," she waved the dripping snake tail about two inches from Parry's face, then did the same to me. Gardener held back until she stuck the remains to one of the porch columns with her pocket knife. "I found that little devil tryin' to sneak into my house and live under the settee with all them other vermin," she explained.

"Ruby," Parry spoke his words very slowly and distinctly, "we've been over this before. There ain't no snakes or rats under your sofa. I've looked."

"They hide when you show up. Snakes ain't dumb, Parry."

"Yes'm."

Ruby turned away from us and started to walk up the porch steps. "I don't know what I'm gonna do about'em," she muttered more to herself than us. "Lord knows Peter can't do nothin'. He's deathly afraid of snakes. Well, come on in ya'll. I'll fix up some tea and dinner."

According to Parry, Peter Krauss was Ruby's dead fiancé. Parry wasn't ever real sure of the story, but he gathered that Peter had been one of the mill workers ("though," Parry was always quick to point out, "he *was* an overseer or foreman or something, so at least he wasn't exactly a common laborer"). Now Old Man O'Neal, I'm sure, didn't cotton with his daughter steppin' out with one of his employees, especially someone on the production line, foreman or no. Parry was sure there was some kind of bad blood about that. As to what happened to the fiancé, I don't rightly know, but I sure as hell can guess that Mr. O'Neal wasn't too pleased to hear of the impending nuptials.

"All's I know for sure," Parry explained to us, "was that part of the fiancé was found up on the roof of the mill, and the head was found down on the ground. They also apparently found one of the fire-axes with blood on it."

"They ever find out who did it?" I asked.

"Not really, but most of the townspeople figured it was Old Man O'Neal, course they never could find enough evidence."

"What do you mean 'not enough evidence'?" Gardener asked, "Didn't they check for fingerprints or something? Match blood types?"

"Gardener, do you have to study to be that stupid? This was 1910; they prob'ly didn't test for fingerprints back then. Hell, I bet they didn't even know what fingerprints were."

Gardener leaned forward with a gleam in his eye. "Did they lynch the old man? I bet they strung him up on that old oak tree in the middle of town. That's where I'd've done it."

"Come on, Gardener," Parry sighed. "Of course they didn't hang the man. It ain't like he killed some Confederate hero or something. We're only talking about some poor white trash immigrant day-laborer. Nobody in their right mind would've lynched a gentleman like O'Neal over something that petty."

"I would have. I think it'd be neat to see the old bastard swing."

Now Miss Ruby didn't say much more about Peter during that first meeting. She just took us into her kitchen, which was basically a large closet with one of them camp stoves and a bathroom sink. She had an old timey icebox (you know, the kind with a huge chunk of ice inside to keep everything cold: *ice* box?). Anyway, she took out some milk from that and cooked up some Campbell's on the camp stove. Then she set four bowls out and dished up the soup.

"What about Peter?" Gardener asked, throwing me a wink.

Ruby dropped the ladle into the pot and turned to stare Gardener down. "What did you say?"

"You only got four bowls out. Ain't Peter gonna eat?"

Ruby looked at Gardener like he was one of the snakes under her sofa and didn't say anything for a long time. Parry looked like he wanted to crawl out the front door, and I felt like even that was too much trouble and just wanted to sink right through the cracks of her warped wood floor. Finally, she turned away from Gardener, who had stared right back at her like Lucifer staring God Almighty back over the fence 'twixt

Heaven and Hell. She picked up the ladle and finished serving up the soup.

"No," she said distantly, "he ain't hungry. He ain't hungry at all. Now eat your soup, and I believe y'all need to be heading on up the road. I thank you, Parry, for the visit. Tell your Momma I appreciate the vegetables."

After this first meeting, Gardener got more and more interested in Ruby. "I like that old lady," he'd say with a laugh. "You're right, Parry. They don't make 'em much crazier than that."

He took to devising all these little pranks we could pull on her. Once he called her up and pretended to be a drug enforcement agent. He told her that drug dealers in the next house over were using her phone line to make their deals and that the GBI needed to tap her line to catch them.

"Yessir," she agreed. "Somethin's got to be done about all these drugs out here. Anything I can do to help."

"Well, ma'am," Gardener said in his best government official voice. "It's pretty simple really; all's we need you to do is to not use your phone until we call you back to say it's okay. Not at all, don't call anyone or answer the phone, or else the suspects'll get hip to the trace. I cannot reemphasize enough, if your voice shows up on our tapes, you may be implicated. So, don't use the phone until we call you back."

"Yessir, don't you worry. I'll do it."

About two weeks later he called her back, and scolded her for answering the phone. "I warned you to leave the phone alone, Miss O'Neal."

"I thought you were going to call me back, but you didn't."

"Well, it's not time to take the trace off yet. But since I got you on the phone, you may as well know."

"Know what?"

Gardener lowered his voice real quiet like. "We suspect the suspects may suspect we suspect them."

"Huh?"

"The gig is up. They think you turned them in."

"Well, what in God's great name are you people goin' to do about this?"

"Calm down, Miss O'Neal. Calm down. We have everything under control. I've got people watching them as we speak. They can't do nothin' without us knowing about it."

"Well, that's good. What are they doing now?"

"Not much ma'am. Not now. But they just got through placing land mines in your daylilies, and maybe even in your yard. See how good we're keeping our eyes on'em?"

"Land mines? What am I goin' to do about my yard?"

"Well, ma'am, I don't think it's a good idea to do too much in your yard at all. Don't worry though; we have everything under control. Just stay in your house. Don't answer the door until we come by to let you know it's safe, and don't answer your phone until we call you back to tell you it's okay. Okay?"

"And you'll take the land mines out of my flower beds and my yard?"

"Yes ma'am. Just don't leave your house and don't answer the phone."

In addition to playing these practical jokes on Miss Ruby, Gardener did everything he could to find out more about her. He questioned Parry, but Parry didn't know much more than what he'd already told us. He began asking the older people in Owen about her, but they couldn't tell much more than Parry. Even Old Skunk Wilson, who knew almost everything about the town there was to know didn't even know Ruby had courted Peter.

"Naw, suh," he said, his old black face scrunched up like he was trying to squeeze his memories out of his ears. "You boys got yer facts all wrong. I don't believe t'was Miss Ruby what was courting that Kraut boy at all. I recollect that it was Rosie, Ruby's sister. But, hell, ain't no need to take my word fer it; I been known to be wrong once er twice. 'Specially now as my mem'ry ain't as sharp as it was. Coulda been Ruby. But Rosie or

Ruby, I sure felt for her when their daddy kilt that boy. I s'pose I thought it were Rosie 'cause that's about the time she left town. But, hell, I reckon growin up with Marst O'Neal'd be just about enough to make anybody leave."

"Do you remember when it was?" Gardener asked. "When Mr. O'Neal killed him?"

"Oh yes," Skunk had this habit of nodding his head as he talked, "If'n I 'member right it was back in ten, when that comet came through. I 'member 'cause I heard about it the mornin' after I saw Halley fly by. Yep, nineteen and ten. You know they say a man can only see that thing once in his life, but I git to see it twice. Not many can claim that. Naw sir."

For a while Gardener gave up on trying to find out any more about Ruby's affair with Peter. I guess he felt he'd exhausted all his sources. I told him to look in the old newspapers at the library, but that idea was so much "mamby pamby boring bullshit."

"If I gotta do research in a stuffy ol' library," he complained. "I may as well be back in school."

So, for the time being, Gardener grew bored with Ruby, and Parry tried to keep the subject from coming up as much as he could. Unfortunately, he couldn't keep the subject dead forever. One Saturday we asked Parry to come up in the mountains with us to try and see the comet.

"It'll be great!" Gardener exclaimed. "We got us some liquor, and some beer, and some grass, and ain't none of us gotta be anywhere 'til Monday. Come on go with us."

"I can't."

"Why the hell not?"

"I just can't, that's all. I got stuff to do this weekend."

"Like what?"

"Personal stuff."

"What kind of personal stuff?"

"My own."

Well, he and Gardener beat each other around the bush like

this for about ten minutes 'til Parry finally broke down and told him. "Oh, Jesus, Gardener. I got to take Ruby up to Atlanta to see a shrink. The whole family's gotta go so I can't get out of it."

I leaned in a little. "Why you takin' Ruby to the shrink, Parry?"

"'Cause she's got it into her lame head that drug dealers are tapping her phone and government agents have planted bombs in her yard, and we can't get her to open her door or answer the phone. All she'll do when we come by to check on her is yell out a window for us to stay out of the daylilies." He looked hard at Gardener, but Gardener didn't miss a beat.

"Aw, gee, Parry," he said. "That's too bad. If there's anything I can do, feel free to ask."

"No, Gardener, I believe you've done more than enough for Ruby. Thanks."

After Parry left, Gardener jumped up from his seat. "Well, my boy," he announced, "it appears like we've had a change in plans."

"I don't see why," I countered. "Just because Parry can't go with us don't mean we can't go camping just the same."

"Oh, I'm afraid it does. You see, Ruby's going to be out of her house for at least a day or two." He winked at me. "And somebody's gotta look after Mr. Krauss. Besides, I wanna see what's in that room."

Even shotgun shacks look creepy after dark. Especially Ruby's perched so precariously on that bluff as it was. Gardener didn't seem to get fazed, but I got the willies just thinkin' about it. The faded white paint almost glowed in the dark, and the places where the paint had peeled... Well, I swear they looked like dripping blood. I almost turned around right then, but I figured if Gardener could handle it, I damn sure could (or at least I damn sure wasn't about to let on that I couldn't).

Her house was unbelievably easy to get into; she'd left her door unlocked. When we got inside her foyer, Gardener took two flashlights out of his pack and held one out to me.

"I don't want to turn on the lights in case the neighbors know she ain't home," he whispered.

"Aw," I tried to joke, "they'd just think it was Peter gettin' up for a snack."

Gardener just snorted and moved down the hall. When he got to "Peter's" room, he stopped and began digging around in his pack.

"What're you doing, Gardener? Just go on in."

"Ain't you ever read Faulkner, boy?" he said without looking up. "She may not'a been lyin' when she told Mr. Beaumont Peter slept here. These crazy old bats do that shit all the time."

I looked at Gardener with renewed wonder; who'd have thought Gardener Smith, of all people, would read, and Faulkner at that. "Gardener," I said, "you just keep unfolding like a flower."

"Ah," he sighed ignoring me, "here they are." He pulled out two paper shop masks (you know, the kind with a little rubber band running around the back to keep it on your head) and handed one to me. "Well," he said as he opened the door, "here we go."

Other than a shit load of dust, the room was just like any other room. There wasn't a dead man on the bed; there wasn't even a very *old* man on the bed. There *was*, however, a man's suit in the closet and a pair of shoes on the floor. Gardener seemed disappointed. He looked all over that room for something, anything, out of the ordinary, and all he found were the clothes. He even looked under the bed, as if the old lady might have stashed Krauss' body there.

"Man," he complained, "I thought for sure she'd've had the head somewhere."

I glanced at him with a questioning look on my face, which he probably couldn't see anyway and turned back to the desk. There wasn't anything on top of it, so I pulled out the chair and began looking through the drawers.

"Hey!" I almost yelled in triumph as I pulled out a bundle of old letters. "Look what I found!"

Gardener rushed over and grabbed one and patted me on the back. "Well, my boy, I knew you were good for something. What've we got here?" He pulled the letter out of its envelope and turned the flashlight on it. "'Mine Leebchin?' What the shit is this?"

"German," I replied looking at one of my own, "I took some last year."

"Well, perfessor? Can you read it?"

"Just a little, I only got a 'C.' Really only a sentence or two. Nothing that'll help us. 'Ich liebe dich und keine andere.' 'I love you and none other.'"

"Well, that's mighty kind of you, but it don't really help us. What else can you find in there?" He began pawing through the drawers himself and pulled out an old leather bound book secured with a clasp. "I do believe," he held it up to me, "that this is her diary. We've hit the jackpot."

As he pulled out his pocketknife and jimmied the clasp, I looked in another drawer and found some old newspaper clippings: "Mysterious Murder at Mill," one read.

"Hey Gardener, listen to this," I began reading the article. "It's dated May 17, 1910: 'The body of Peter Krauss, local laborer, was discovered atop O'Neal and Co.'s Cotton Mill this morning by workers... blah, blah, blah ... decapitated ... person or persons unknown, using a fire axe as a weapon ... blah, blah ... head and bloodstained axe found in bushes below... Authorities baffled... No leads."

Another headline read: "O'Neal Questioned in Krauss' Death." The next: "O'Neal Cleared of Charges, Death Ruled Accidental."

"Yeah," Gardener chuckled, "his head accidentally got in the way of the axe. Listen to this, it's the old lady's diary: 'Peter said he loved me today. I can't believe my fortune! I sit here in my room looking out at the comet. I believe it's a sign that our love will last until we see Halley again. Peter says he'll take care of his "other problem" as soon as he possibly can. Oh God, let it be soon! As soon as he clears his "other problem" up, he'll ask daddy for my hand, but even if daddy forbids it, we are to be married by Saturday.' That's dated May 10, 1910." He flipped a few pages. "Okay, May 15: 'It may be too early to tell, yet, but I felt a kick this morning before the sickness. I must tell Peter, he'll be so happy. He's such a darling.'"

"Well, well," I chuckled, "I just bet he is."

Gardener continued reading, "'Later: Peter is as proud as a peacock. How he struts! He told me that his "other problem" is taken care of, though not as cleanly as he had hoped, and he will speak to father tonight. I am to meet him tomorrow night atop the mill. It's supposed to be the night Halley is brightest. I believe this, too, is a sign. Our love will shine just as bright if not brighter. Oh, blessed Halley, I thank you for your fortune.'" Gardener stopped.

"Well," I said. "What's next?"

"That's all she wrote," he flipped a few more pages and put it back into the drawer. "It's quite a story though, you gotta admit that. So old Ruby got knocked up, Goddamn, that's funny." Gardener started laughing to beat all hell, but suddenly, I didn't think it was all that humorous. All I could think about was poor old Ruby, and how she must have felt when she lost Peter. I assumed she had to have been there when it happened. No wonder she moved out here to the mill village. I wondered what happened to the child. Probably had to have it "taken care of" by a midwife or something. The whole story kind of made me sad.

I thought about Peter's "other problem" and what that could have been. Was he in debt? Wanted? Married? Then I remembered Skunk, and I knew he was right about Rosie seein' Peter. She had. It was the only thing that made sense. She'd been seein' Peter on the side, and he had to break it off with her to marry Ruby. I knew, now, why Rosie had left town, too. She had killed Peter. So the old man really was innocent.

"Come on, Gardener," I said. "We better be headin' on out."

When we got to the road Gardener turned around. "Hold on," he said as he scrambled back up the bluff. "I forgot something. Be right back."

When he returned, his pack was significantly larger.

Ruby was gone nearly a week; she came back the following Thursday. That next Saturday was May 16. It was also, once again, the night Halley's Comet would be its brightest. Gardener just couldn't pass up such a "golden opportunity to play with Ruby some more."

"Oh come on, Gardener," I said. "Can't you leave the old lady alone now? It's really getting old."

"I promise you," he replied with a grin, "that this'll be the last time. I swear it. The last time."

I had done more than just grow tired of playing juvenile jokes on a senile old lady. I began to feel a little ashamed of it. I mean, the lady was damn near a hundred, and apart from being a little touched in the head, Ruby was just like anybody else, nicer than most, even.

I felt that she'd been wronged throughout most of her life. Her fiancé been killed, by her own sister, while she was pregnant with his child. She probably had to get rid of the kid either by abortion or adoption. She'd had to leave home when she was about sixteen. I just thought she'd been through enough.

I didn't understand why Gardener felt so damned intent on pestering the old lady. To this day, I don't understand it. It was as if he felt Ruby had sinned against him personally, like her sleeping with Peter Krauss, three quarters of a century ago, had been a personal slap in his face, and he was going to make her pay for it. At that moment, I dreaded the day he would have a girl cheat on him. I dreaded it with all my heart, for I knew with a certainty bordering on the religious that he would do something bad. That he couldn't help himself. I knew, too, that there'd be nothing I could do about it, even if I knew about it.

I'd never done anything in my life. I had never once made a decisive action, or followed through on a decision. I was a watcher, always had been. The world was my television, and I was a couch potato. I knew this and had long since come to grips with it. Others acted, and I observed. Just this once, though, I knew I had to do something. Gardener couldn't be allowed to pester Ruby anymore. Yet, I realized there'd be no swaying him once his mind was set. So I decided to warn Ruby myself.

It was around dusk Saturday that I made it to her house. I figured Gardener, with his flair for the dramatic, would wait until full dark, probably midnight, before he'd do anything. I'd have plenty of time to warn her. I found her sitting in a cane rocker on her front porch. She was gazing off into the sky, chewing, and spitting tobacco juice into a paper cup. She stared so intently at the evening sky, I didn't think she'd noticed me. I was just about to announce myself when she turned to me and stared into my eyes.

Her stare was penetrating. It was like she gazed straight into my soul, and she wouldn't speak 'til she found out what was in there. Finally, she spit some juice into her cup.

"Well, boy, may's well git on up here." She pulled another rocker over with her toe. "Have a seat. We got business, you and me."

Her voice surprised me. Not her words, really, but her voice. It was so clear and determined. Not at all like the quavering senile voice she'd used all the other times before. She was a completely different person (not sane, really, but more lucid), and I didn't know whether to attribute it to the head shrinking she'd just returned from or to the date and circumstances. I sat in the proffered chair and didn't say anything.

She turned towards me again. "You and that other boy," she said, "y'all must hate me somethin' awful to treat me like you do. Or think me a complete moron. One or both."

"No ma'am, I... "

"Didn't your daddy ever teach you to speak your turn? It ain't polite to interrupt, especially your elders. And I reckon I'm about the elderest of'em all. Funny though, nobody's ever given me a chance to speak."

There was a silence for quite a while. She seemed to be thinking, and I was, quite frankly, scared to death.

"I loved that man, you know. I'd've done anything for him. I did a lot more'n I should have. Things ladies don't do. Oh, Poppa despised him, 'cause he knew about the things we did. I didn't care though; I loved him and that was the way it had to be." She looked up into the sky again. "He loved me, too; I don't care what anybody else said. It was ME he loved and no other. Sure, she was a problem, but it shouldn't've been nothin' the two of us couldn't've handled. He did love me. It's vital that you know that. 'Cause with love all things are possible.

"We could've worked it out. We could have. He said we'd had a good run, but it was time to move on. I thought it was just 'cause Poppa'd been giving him heat about our doings, and he was scared. I knew Poppa had connections. I knew he could get anything, ANYTHING, he wanted done. He'd had things done before. 'It's the Southern way,' he'd brag. 'My friends do things for me, and I do things for my friends.' So, I figured Poppa or his friends had finally gotten to Peter. But he DID love me. He did."

She quieted down again, and I found the courage to speak up. "What happened to the baby?"

She looked at me, "What baby? There warn't no baby. Just me and him and our doings. Didn't no baby come of all that." She grew silent and thoughtful. After a second she turned around and slapped my face. It didn't hurt at all, the old lady was at an awkward angle and didn't have much strength left in her arm anyway, I imagine. But it startled me all the same.

"You saw the book." she seethed. "Didn't you? You saw it. Well let me tell you this much, buddy boy. That book ain't naught but lies. Rose never knew the half of it."

"Rose?"

"It was ME he loved. ME!! Not Rose. Oh, she oohed and aahed over him like he was God come down from on high, but he saw through that. He loved ME!! Do you understand?"

"Yes'm," I replied slowly. "I believe I understand just fine."

"Then you don't need to be told," she smiled and nodded, smiled and rocked contentedly. She looked out to the sky. It was dark now, and she pointed to the comet making its way across the sky. "That was our sign," she said. "Peter said it symbolized his love for me, eternally circling. I was his universe. He loved ME, and no other. He wrote that to ME, not her. ME.

"When he finally told me about Rose, I cried and screamed and hit him. How could he do that to me? After I did things for him ladies didn't do? He just turned away from me and left. Well, heh, I followed him. I wanted to apologize. I knew Rose could get rid of the little bastard, and when she did that, Peter would be free to elope with me. I knew that he didn't *really* want to marry her. It was just the honorable thing. So I followed him to make him understand.

"But when he got to the roof, and SHE was there, SHE made him say things. He didn't love her, but he said he did. I knew it was just because she was big with his child. I knew he loved ME and no other. But when she made him do things on that roof... When she did those same things with him I did. I knew I had to fix it. Things had gotten out of hand, and cooler heads had to prevail. So I fixed things right."

"*You* killed him?" I felt as if the ground had slipped out from under me. "*You* killed Peter? What about Rose? What happened to Rose?"

"Her, I killed. I killed her and her lying tongue and her little bastard. I had to. He was getting too carried away, and I was afraid he'd forget about us. I had to kill her, so I did. I buried her over there." She pointed to the grove of trees separating her backyard from the wilderness. "I moved out here to make sure she didn't come back to bother us.

"But I never killed Peter. Ain't you heard a thing I been sayin'? Peter ain't dead. He's the comet, he's comin' back for me. He just needed to cool off and gather himself together. Our love is eternal, and he's coming back tonight. Oh, I hit him on the head, but that was just to knock some sense into him. That's all. He's coming back tonight."

She sat and rocked and nodded and rocked some more. I got up and walked away. As I looked up on her porch, I saw her gazing at the comet with a smile on her face and humming to herself. I turned away and climbed back down the bluff not noticing the shadow moving up her drive, so intent I was on my own thoughts.

We have always, I thought, associated comets with great events. Wise men and shepherds gathered around the Christ child to worship after seeing an unusually bright star in the east (historians tell us this was Halley's Comet). The Emperor Constantine, we're told, converted to Christianity after witnessing the Holy Cross flying across the evening sky before a battle (historians tell us that this, too, was Halley's Comet). Mark Twain came into this world with Halley's Comet in the year 1835 and died with the comet as well in 1910. And I had just learned that not only had Ruby killed both her sister and her lover the night of the comet, but she believed that the lover would return to her on this night, riding in from regions unknown on the tail of the selfsame comet. I mean everybody makes a big deal out of comets. People just go crazy over them.

I didn't know how I felt about all this. On one hand it seemed so much hogwash. I mean, wasn't this the same shit all them whacked-out hippies preached about? And we all know how full of it they are. Some people have been known to kill themselves over comets; I'll never understand that (as if there weren't better things to kill yourself over). But on the other hand, I mean, the facts held up these beliefs most of the time. Who was I to say they were wrong? Except I really doubted Peter Krauss would be around to catch up with Ruby tonight (or any other night for that matter).

As I slowly made my way back home, I remembered the shadow on Ruby's drive, and it occurred to me that I hadn't warned Ruby about Gardener.

Parry found the body the next morning. She had fallen off her porch and broken her neck. He sat on my porch drinking a beer and telling us about it as Gardener sat smugly against the wall smoking a cigarette. "I swear to you," Parry said. "I never seen a face like hers. There wasn't a wrinkle on the thing. It was all stretched, and her eyes were so wide I thought they'd popped out. Y'all, she looked like she'd seen a ghost."

He took a swallow of beer and shook his head. "You know, I guess I will miss the old bat, though."

Gardener stood up and walked over to him. He put his hand on Parry's shoulder, "Aw, gee, Parry," he said. "That's too bad. If there's anything I can do, feel free to ask."

Parry just looked right into his eyes, like he was God Almighty starin' Lucifer back. "No, Gardener, I believe you've done more than enough for Ruby. Thanks."

III. Hell's Ditch

When Emily Blanchard turned fifteen, she lied about her age and got a job waitressing at Hell's Ditch, the all-night diner run by Big Bob Crumb. I wasn't too sure how I felt about it, but it ain't like I had much of a say in the matter. See, I was just her "landlord," so to speak. The arrangement was, and always had been, that she'd stay in my place, the old slave shack in the woods, rent free, and in return she'd keep the place up. I wasn't never her advisor or counselor or parent, or nothing. Besides, I lived about a mile away with my dad; what did I know about what all needed to get taken care of to live in a place alone?

"Look, buddy," she said to me when I voiced some misgivings about her working (you know things like youth labor laws, perjury, and just plain dishonesty, little shit like that), "a girl's got to eat, and I ain't never been too good at hunting, and I sure as hell cain't skin or clean nothing worth a damn. Big Bob'll let me work for meals and a little spending money. You cain't give me that. You ain't even told your daddy about my bein' out here, and it's been almost a year."

I had to admit she had a point. I couldn't provide for her. "And there ain't no need for you to," Gardener'd say. "Hell, she's a big girl; she can make out all right on her own," and he'd grin that grin that'd make my stomach sink. I wasn't sure what their relationship was, but I felt Gardener knew a little more about Emily than I was comfortable knowing he knew.

As for myself, it was also true I hadn't told Dad about Emily, but mainly 'because I figured he'd first crawl my butt because I was still hanging out in that "feeble excuse for a shithouse shack," and then he'd start kidding me about "keeping a young lady." If I wasn't sure about Gardener's relationship with Emily, I was damn sure about my own relationship with her: at best, friends; at worst, erstwhile landlord and tenant. I mean, what can a guy expect from a girl two years younger than him in age but about twenty years older in experience and attitude?

So why didn't I just leave her to her shack and her job and get while the getting was good? Who knows? I know I was afraid for her, and I knew nothing good could come of working in that greasy spoon truck stop.

"It ain't like I'm sellin' my soul to the Devil," she explained. "I'm a waitress; I take orders and deliver them. My God, you act like I've been hired by some kinda perverted greasy slime ball. It's Big Bob for Christ's sake."

Hell, I thought "perverted greasy slime ball" summed Big Bob pretty much up. Robert Crumb looked like one huge massive lard ass shoved into a sleeveless T-shirt and dungaree pants until both looked like they'd about blow. His long greasy hair hung down his back in a ponytail almost but not quite (unfortunately) hiding the crack of his ass peeking out of his beltless trouser waist. He always had this half chewed unlit cigar butt hanging out of his mouth when he cooked. I never could figure out why the health department didn't condemn him, much less his eating establishment.

As for Hell's Ditch, what can I say but that Big Bertha, Bob's sister (imagine Bob with different plumbing), worked there and frequently took her "regulars" back into the kitchen for the "Daily Special." Just ask Gardener what that "special" consisted of; it was only last year when he considered himself one of the regularest of the regulars. But I couldn't tell Emily any of this. Ladies don't need to hear about such filth, and she *was* a lady, Blanchard or no.

Of course, Gardener would argue that her "Blanchardness" implied that she was familiar with such filth.

"All the more reason for me not to tell her about it," I'd reply.

So Emily started working for Big Bob, and I had to just bite the bullet and wait for her to quit. In the meantime, I had my own problems to worry about. I was seventeen years old, and I still hadn't "known" a woman. I wasn't real sure what the problem was; I mean, I didn't stink or nothing. I was reasonably attractive; I damn sure wasn't no Bob Crumb, and he seemed to be getting plenty (go figure). At first, I figured maybe there was a streak of celibacy running through the school, but Parry was quick to point out that we had one of the highest teen pregnancy rates in the county.

"So either girls're still sayin' yes," he theorized, "or we're in for one Hell of a Second Coming."

So I was baffled. I couldn't seem to even get a girl to go out with me, much less spend the night with me.

"Hell, boy," Gardener'd say, "you don't need a whole night, for Christ's sake. It don't take but a few minutes."

Now, Gardener'd tried numerous times to set me up with what he referred to as "sure shots," but they inevitably fired blanks. After he gave up in disgust, Parry stepped in to try his hand.

"You don't need to be listening to that idiot," Parry explained. "Next thing you know, he'll have you down in the "Ditch" with Bertha. You just can't expect to get lucky on the first date. It's the eighties, man. You gotta romance'em. Work up to it. Take it slow. You can't expect to run home without takin' the bases first. Now, I'm gonna set you up with my second cousin Christine Davis. She oughta be just about right for you."

"Oh, is she easy?"

After I picked myself up off the ground, Parry looked at me real hard. "Yep," he said, wiping his hand on his pants leg, "you sure have been spendin' too much time with that Gardener. As I was sayin', slow and easy, man, slow and easy. Now I'm doin' this against my better judgment, so don't let me down."

Well, before I could say yay or nay to this whole blind date business, Parry had already turned around and walked off, pausing only long enough to tell me that he'd set it all up for Friday night at Lin Po's Pizza Pagoda.

The Pizza Pagoda was the local pizza joint. It was owned by

the Wangs, a Chinese couple who couldn't seem to hack it in either the laundry or the restaurant businesses until Lin Po Wang, the husband, decided what the town of Owen really needed was a Chinese pizza palace. So he got a job at the Pizza Inn over in Caton and studied their methods diligently. After he felt he had learned enough and could hand toss a crust with the big boys, Lin Po bought this old warehouse up by the interstate and opened his eatery.

At the Pizza Pagoda, you could get just about anything on your pizza except pepperoni (which Lin Po was leery of, being too expensive to risk losing money on). They had pineapple pizza, sweet and sour pizza (pork, beef, and chicken), and even fortune pizza (though this delicacy was short lived due to the rash of complaints about the greasy little papers sticking in between people's teeth). Strangely enough, Lin Po had found his niche.

I looked at my watch (8:45) and then glanced over at Parry as I tossed a few appetizer noodles into my mouth.

"What time'd you say they'd meet us?" I asked.

"Well," Parry replied, "Christy said she had to pick Kate up at seven, and they should be here by 8:30."

"How's it take an hour and a half to get three miles away?"

"I don't know, maybe they have to put their faces on together or somethin'. Girl shit, man, don't ask."

Parry had tried to set up just a regular blind date for me and Christy, but she felt leery about trusting his judgment on a guy (I'm not sure, but I think maybe the last fella he set her up with turned out to be some kind of car thief or rapist or murderer or one of them computer programmers). She told him she'd only go out with me if he went along as a double date for this Kate girl.

"This'll be even better," Parry assured me. "Now you can watch a *real* pro at work and follow my lead. Gardener's been leadin' you astray for far too long, and I ain't real sure you're quite ready to be set loose to fly solo."

Emily had seemed leery of the whole deal. She'd been working for Big Bob for about a month by the time Parry suggested this date with his cousin. I swung by the shack the day after he set up the whole deal to see what she'd say.

I found her asleep on the porch at about four o'clock in the afternoon, and it took forever for her to wake up. She rose groggily to sit on the edge of the porch with her feet dangling off. Her speech was real slurred, from sleepiness I reckon, when I told her about my impending date.

"I don't like it," she said. "Not one bit. I mean, Parry's nice'n all, but what do you *really* know about him? What do you really know about this girl, either? Take it from me, buddy boy; you don't know shit about shit. I mean you cain't know nobody 'til you've spent *quality* time with them." The way she said "quality" made me feel weird, like I should've been ashamed or something. "You don't know thing one," she continued, "about what's out there. I mean this girl could be some kinda freak or psycho or somethin'. It's a bad world, boy, and you ain't even prepared for it. Now you might oughta leave so's I can get ready to work."

I asked her how work was. She gave a hollow chuckle. "Fine," she said. "Just fine. Regular."

As I walked away from the shack, I couldn't help but feel like there was something I was missing in that whole conversation. But I couldn't for the life of me figure out what it was.

So here I was, at Lin Po's Pizza Pagoda with Parry, eating stale Chinese noodles, waiting for Christine and Kate to show up, and (truth be known) kind of hoping they wouldn't. Maybe Emily was right and she was some kind of freak show psycho. I mean, if she was as great as Parry insisted she was, why wasn't she already seeing somebody? Maybe I wasn't ready to go out with somebody yet. Maybe she was butt-ugly, and I'd have to pretend to be interested in her most of the evening. Why didn't I just leave and go over to Hell's Ditch and visit with Emily a while? I was about to do just this when they sat down next to us at the table.

Now when one of your friends tells you he's got a second cousin who's "just right" for you, we all know not to expect too much. I mean, if she was half as great as he claimed, hell, he'd be going out with her his own self. Second cousins are, after all, legal. So I wasn't really looking for any kind of beauty queen or nothing. I'd've just been happy if this girl was under two hundred pounds. What I really wanted was for this evening to get over with so I could run along home and get back to all that important nothing I had to do there.

Christine Davis was drop dead gorgeous. A blonde bombshell with a body that wouldn't quit. She wore her hair in a ponytail in the back, and she had the biggest, bluest eyes I'd ever seen. I took one look at her and realized there wasn't no way in hell she'd ever be interested in a skinny pimply-faced moron like myself.

"Dammit, Christy," Parry said as the girls sat down, "y'all were s'posed to be here half an hour ago. We were just about to give up on you."

"Now, Parry," she returned, "don't get your boxers all in a wad. We got lost, but we're here now, so there ain't no call for you gettin' all upset. Let's just order us some food and get goin'." She turned and smiled at me. "You must be my date. I'm Christy."

I couldn't hardly get my breath up to speak, but I finally managed to tell her my name although I stuttered something awful.

She turned back to her cousin. "Well Parry, this here's Kate. Kate, Parry."

They smiled at each other but didn't speak. I got the distinct feeling that Kate was less than pleased to be there. I figured Christy, too, was just making small talk to get the evening over with.

I began to think Emily may have been right. I *wasn't* ready for this. I *was* out of my league here. I didn't hardly know nobody here. I mean, I'd really only known Parry a few months. I really didn't belong here, and I may as well face it: I'd've done much better just to stay home.

I looked at Christy sitting next to me, though, and I thought I felt her thigh rubbing up next to mine as she alternately leaned forward to talk to Parry and then sat back, so I figured, *What the hell? I may's well enjoy it. What can it hurt?*

Now Kate Crawford, she was a different story altogether. You ever meet somebody you thought was drop dead gorgeous right up until they opened their mouth? Well, that was Kate all over. I mean, she couldn't hold no candle to Christy, but she *was* damned attractive. She had this long brown hair that just went on forever. And her figure, my God, that girl could've made a blind man blush.

But she had this voice. One of them naturally whiny voices with a thick redneck twang, and every time she'd open her mouth she'd let out this sigh as if in her sixteen years, she'd seen all in the world there was to see and lived all the things there was to live and didn't none of it measure up to her expectations. (Still, her daddy called her "Pumpkin.") All she did was complain, and I don't think nothing on God's green Earth could've been good enough for her.

"(Sigh) ... What kind of dip-wad place is this?" she asked when she looked at the menu. "What's a Chow Mien Pizza? I don't want to eat nowhere they ain't got a hamburger or a real pizza."

Parry looked at her. "Well, is there any place you'd like to go?"

"(Sigh) ... Any place would be better'n here. A greasy spoon diner would be better'n this rat-hole dump. I hate this place."

When we walked into Hell's Ditch, I knew we wouldn't be staying long. Kate took one whiff of the place, and that nose of hers just began creeping on up her face.

"Hey, there's Gardener," I announced to postpone the inevitable whine. We went over to his table. "What're you doin' here?" I asked after we'd made our introductions and sat down.

"I got a little business to take care of with Emily," he replied, giving me that wink I hated so much. "I gotta ask her for some money."

Parry reached into his pocket and handed him a five. "Here, take this. Ain't no need in you borrowin' money from a girl strugglin' to make her way."

"Don't need to borrow no money," Gardener returned, stuffing the five into his pocket. "She owes me it. Much obliged though."

"This her table?" I asked looking around. "Where is she?"

"She's busy in the back. But I reckon she'll be out directly."

"(Sigh) ... I'm ready to order." Kate interjected. "I'm so hongry, I could jest die."

Parry rolled his eyes and looked like he wished she *would* just die, but he turned to Big Bob over at the grill instead. "Hey Bob, how 'bout some burgers or somethin' over here?"

Bob glared over at our table and pushed a greasy strand of hair out of his eyes while flicking his cigar butt off somewhere in the vicinity of his ashtray. "This is my place, boys, and I don't take no orders from nobody but my waitresses, so I'll kindly ask you not to shout out at me like I was some field hand." Then he yelled into the back of the diner. "Emily, get your ass out here if you want to keep workin'! You got orders to take. Do that shit on your own time!"

Now I don't mind telling you, I got a little pissed at Bob for yelling at Emily thattaway. I mean, there ain't no call for hollering at nobody when they've most likely been working their ass off all night and want to take a little break. I'd a good mind to tell him so, but I knew he could probably break me half in two without thinking twice about it. He'd done it to other people for less. So, I figured I better head on back to the johns and cool off a little before I got myself into a fix I couldn't really get myself out of.

As I got up from the table, Emily walked out of the back rearranging her dress and patting down her hair. I was so busy noticing her, I almost ran down some big fat-ass redneck cowboy who was coming out of the bathroom area about the same time, smelling something sinful and smiling at Emily in a way I didn't at all think was respectful.

"Hey pal, watch where yer runnin'," he growled as I ducked to keep from hitting him.

When I got back, Parry and the girls were getting up from the table, Kate looking disgusted and Christy and Parry just looking tired.

Christy put her arm around my neck and leaned towards my head; she smelled almost as good as she looked. I don't know what kind of perfume she had on, but I ain't never smelled any on anybody since that smelled quite as nice. "They don't have french fries," she whispered. "She won't eat anywhere that don't carry french fries. I really am sorry to be such trouble, but we need to find someplace else to eat before she has some kind of fit."

"(Sigh) ... Well, whoever heard of a burger place not havin' no fries?" she whined. "Nobody can eat a hamburger without fries. It just ain't right."

Emily was leaning over, explaining to Gardener that she hadn't been paid yet, but she'd have him some money before her shift was over.

"See that you do, honey pie," he said as we walked out. "See that you do."

The last thing I saw before getting into my car was Gardener patting Emily on her rump and grinning that same dumb-ass grin.

Well, we wound up eating at some overpriced and undercooked steakhouse where Kate proceeded to order every expensive thing on the meal board. Apparently, if you didn't have to mortgage your vital organs to eat it, she didn't figure it was much worth eating. Christy and I made do with a salad between us; by this time I think we had begun to lose our patience with Kate, along with our appetites. Anyways, I was just enjoying being around Christy. She kept rubbing her leg against mine up under the table, even when she wasn't leaning in to speak to Kate or Parry. But every time I'd glance in her direction, she'd just smile politely and turn away, so I knew it had to just be on account of the small booth and all.

Parry got the "All You Can Eat Spare-Rib Special" and proceeded to gnaw'em down to the bone and further, making all kinds of a racket. Slurping and slobbering and sucking. At one point he even broke one of the bones, glanced at Kate, and slurped the marrow.

Kate just sighed loudly and nibbled at her T-bone steak with ribeyes on the side; baked potato with sour cream, butter, *and* bacon; rolls; chef's salad; broccoli and cheese; peas and carrots; and ice cream swirl; and then sipped at her ice tea, coffee, water, and Sprite.

As for me, I was sure I was striking out with Christy almost as much as Kate was striking out with Parry. She hadn't said much more than three or four words to me since she introduced herself at Lin Po's. Sometimes I'd catch her staring at me with this look of bewilderment, and I just knew she thought I was some kind of stupid loser. Since I had no idea how to carry on a civilized conversation with her, I just ate my salad and hoped that the night would end quickly.

If my date wasn't bad enough, I had to deal with Kate, too. Now, ordinarily I would've just left Parry to deal with the whiny bitch and taken Christy home. But we were all in my car, and Kate had come with Christy, so there really wasn't no way I could have left without bringing everybody with me anyway. So I continued to sit and eat the salad and hope Kate would keep quiet for just about another hour.

Did I mention she ordered just about everything on the menu? Well, after she had eaten maybe two bites out of half her dishes, she pushed all her plates and bowls aside.

"(Sigh) ... Well," she announced, "that's about all I can hold. Y'all ready to leave yet?"

Parry spit spare-rib across the table into my lap. "What do you mean 'that's about all?' You barely touched your food!"

"(Sigh) ... Well, I guess I just wasn't as hungry as I thought was."

"If I ain't mistaken," he countered, "you were 'so hungry you could jest die.' You got any idea how much that smorgasbord of yours cost? You *are* gonna get a to-go box or somethin' ain't you?"

"(Sigh) ... I don't want to walk out of here with all that food," she whined. "People might think I'm some kinda pig."

"Or other farm animal," I muttered to myself.

Christy almost choked on her water when I said that, so I felt real bad about it and figured I had just about shot my wad with this girl. She looked at her and then spoke real slow. "Kate, honey, don't you realize how much food you're wastin'? There're folks starvin' all over the world, and, you know, Donahue says it just ain't right to go around throwin' food away."

"(Sigh) ... Well, that's Donahue's problem. I ain't hungry no more, and I ain't takin' home no damn doggy bag."

At this both Christy and Parry looked like they'd like nothing more than to strangle the girl right there in the restaurant. I thought it best to get on out of the place before it got any worse. "Well," I said rising from my seat, "I believe we all ought to be headin' on out now. Come on."

When we got outside, I figured we should all call it a night and go on home, but Kate wouldn't have none of that.

"(Sigh) ... I ain't ready to go yet," she complained. "I need to go to the mall. "

"I ain't goin' to no mall," Parry interjected. "It's an hour away, and if I wanted to see a bunch of stuck up snobs and yuppies, I'd go down to the Owen Country Club and save myself the trip."

But Kate threw a fit. "Well, I gotta go to the mall!" she yelled. "And I ain't gonna do a goddamn thing or go no damn where "til we go to the mall! I mean it! I'm goin' to that mall, and that's jest all there is to it!"

Now I don't know what all the big hoopla is over these malls. I ain't never understood it, and I don't reckon I ever will. I mean, I remember when Southfield Mall opened up, about six or seven years before this. I don't believe I ever saw so many stuck-ups and blue-bloods before or since. Everybody crowded around this concrete building with this gigantic ribbon wrapped around it like it was some kind of shrine or church or something. They just stood there waiting for something to happen. I don't know what they wanted. From the looks on their faces, I gathered they were waiting for Jesus to show up with a shopping cart and an American Express card saying, "Come on in, folks. It's all on me."

But the only thing happened was this fella in a tux with this big-ass pair of scissors blathered on and on and on. He kept talking about what a godsend this mall was for the community. That it was gonna save the poverty-stricken by giving them jobs. It was gonna save the wealthy by giving them selection. And it was gonna save the environment on account of all the gas and exhaust it would cut out not having to go into Atlanta every time somebody wanted a pair of slacks and a Norelco. Then he cut the gigantic yellow ribbon, and everybody went on in and shopped until the Grand Opening sales were over. Then they went on back to Atlanta for slacks, the stores cut their inventory and laid off most their workers, and we got this hole in the ozone layer and stuff. The only folks who went there now were the young wannabe yuppies who could afford to buy but couldn't afford to spend all that money on gas to Atlanta and the wannabe-wannabe yuppies whose parents wouldn't let them take the car out of the county limits after sundown.

Oh, and apparently whiny bitches who irritated the piss out

their friends, dates, and complete strangers because we all piled into my little Honda Civic and started out to the mall. Now, I know didn't nobody else want to go the mall, and I sure as hell didn't relish an hour-long trek up the interstate in such confined quarters with Kate. But we all reckoned if we went, she'd shut up and quit her whining. No such luck.

We weren't on the road ten minutes before she started in bitching about the music on the radio.

"(Sigh) ... Who're the Beatles? Can't we listen to somethin' from this century? Put on The Judds or somethin'. Somethin' I can dance to."

"I don't think," I returned, "I don't think anybody better be dancin' in this small-ass car. We're listenin' to the Beatles."

"(Sigh) ... But I don't like the Beatles."

"You hadn't never heard of them 'til now."

"(Sigh) ... Well, I don't like them, now, either. I want to listen to The Judds."

Now I didn't want to make a scene tonight. I really didn't. I tried my damnedest not to, in fact. I think I showed great restraint. But even I have my limits. I pulled the car over into the breakdown lane and turned off the engine before turning around in my seat and fixing her with my iciest stare.

"Let me fill you in on somethin', little girl." I began. "You ain't in charge. Very few people in this world are in charge, and you ain't nowhere near it. You ain't in charge here. I am. You wanna know why?" I waved my keys in her face. "I'm in charge 'cause I got the keys. See? No keys, no power. You ain't got no keys, so you're low bitch on the totem pole. I'm in charge 'cause I can tell the car where to go and you can't."

She just looked at me with a blank stare like a deer in the headlights, but Parry stared at me in amazed respect, and I thought I noticed even Christy smiling at me with, if not interest, at least a little curiosity.

"Now, we're going to the mall," I continued, "To shut you up. But we're listening to the Beatles, and that's all there is to it."

With that and a nonchalant wink at Christy, I flourished the keys one more time and spun back around in my seat. The keys flew out the window and into the highway.

After I had retrieved my keys, avoided being run down by a station wagon, a pick-up truck, and a semi hauling hogs, I returned quietly to the car to find The Judds on the radio, and we went on to the mall.

Of course, by the time we got there, the place had done closed and there wasn't but one car left in the parking lot. Turns out it was Kate's boyfriend, Curtis.

"I had him meet me here in case the date didn't work out," she explained as this mousy little kid glared at Parry from behind her, trying to look tough and sullen, but only succeeding in looking little ... and mousy.

We were all stunned, but Parry was the first to speak. "Well, before you go, I just wanted to thank you for such an enjoyable evening. I mean, I don't know about these two, but I've never felt so special. Maybe we could do it again sometime." He smiled at Curtis and beamed at Kate. "You know, just you, me, your boyfriend..."

After she left, nobody spoke for a long time. Again Parry was the first.

"Christy, why didn't you tell me she had a boyfriend?"

"Who knew?" she replied.

"Who'd want her?" I muttered.

When we dropped Christy off at her car, she asked if I would mind standing with her while she unlocked the door. I said alright and walked around to escort her. Well, she immediately grabbed my hand and pulled me aside.

"I wanted to apologize for the night," she explained as her thumb rubbed against my hand. "I figured Parry'd fixed me up with another stupid loser, and I kinda wanted to turn the tables on him for once. I didn't mean to ruin your night, too, and I'm sorry. If it'd be okay with you, though, I'd like to try it again sometime soon."

Well, you could've knocked me down with a feather duster. "Uh ... yeah," I stammered, "that'd be okay... Um, call me or somethin'. Thanks."

She said, "No problem," and then she pulled me close to her and kissed me. With tongue, even.

About eight the next morning, I knew Emily'd be home from work, so I went on out to the woods, heading for my shack. I wanted to tell her that she was wrong. The world wasn't such a bad place, not really. And Christy wasn't some kind of freak or psycho. I did know shit about shit (at least about some shit), and I knew there wasn't no need in Emily being so damned down all the time. Working third shift at Hell's Ditch couldn't be all that bad, and if it was, maybe she should find another line of work. I was sure she could do something that paid better, if nothing else. I was on top of the world, and I figured everybody else ought to be as well.

About the time I was going in, I saw Gardener coming out of the woods counting a wad of bills. I started to call out to him, but he saw me first and walked towards me.

"Hey, boy," he said as he drew near. "How'd your date go last night?"

"Fair to middlin' I reckon, nothin' special." I didn't want to tell Gardener about Christy, 'cause I knew he'd just turn it around into something stupid, so I changed the subject. I nodded toward his money. "Emily pay up?"

"Yeah," he grinned, "I reckon you could say that."

"That's quite a wad there. How much she owe you?"

Gardener looked at me sharp like he was trying to figure out what I just said. He answered me real guardedly. "Enough," he said and walked off.

By the time I reached the clearing with the shack, I had that same old sinking feeling in my stomach. Emily was sitting on the porch in an old rocking chair I had brought out from my attic for her, and she was wrapped in a blanket, but she hadn't seen me yet. She looked tired. I saw her clothes all crumpled up in the corner. She just kept rocking back and forth, back and forth, like she was thinking real hard about something. As I drew nearer, she never did take any notice of me, but just kept staring blankly out at all the trees and humming this song I could almost, but not quite, remember. I knew it was from some kiddie musical movie, but I just couldn't place it. Something about rainbows.

As I came closer to the porch, she looked at me but never did say anything. She just kept rocking and humming, rocking and humming, and I knew, then, that something *was* wrong with the world. Maybe it really was a bad place, and I *didn't* know shit about shit.

IV. The Dead Bury Their Dead in the House on Top of the World

I reckon every town's got its ghost stories and haunted houses, and Owen, Georgia wasn't no different. I swear we had so many tales of death, murder, suicide, and execution that come Judgment Day, we'd all be in for one hell of a population explosion. It seemed just about every house or barn that was more'n twenty years old had some kind of ghost or spell or curse on it. And half the ones that were less than twenty were built on some kind of battle field, dueling ground, or Indian graveyard. So if you were out for some spooky sightseeing on one fall or winter night, you wouldn't have no trouble trying to find somewhere to go.

I mean there was Parry's Aunt Ruby's place down on Coleman Street. Seemed like all the mill village folks kept talkin' bout how since her death, she and her murdered fiancé'd been knocking around up there all hours of night. Skunk Wilson kept talkin' about this haunt what kept following him around the city park at night.

"He jes' keeps at me, just like my old daddy," Skunk explained. "Ever times I lays my head down on a bench, there he is a clappin' his hands together to beat all hell and yellin'.

"'Git on up, boy!' That's what he keeps sayin'. 'Git on up, boy, times a wastin' and we's got work to do.' Next thing I know, I done been kicked out of that bench, and he's gone. Gettin' so's a body cain't get no kind of sleep out 'n that park at night."

Some folks spoke of disturbances out past the old Civil War battleground. They kept saying how about once or twice a year, all the dead Confederate and Yankee veterans'd get on out of their graves and have another go at the Battle for Owen. Although, I gotta say, me and Gardener and Parry stayed out there all night once when it was supposed to happen, and we didn't see nothing 'cept for a couple cats in heat and three or four dogs riled up and growlin' over some dead animal they'd dug up somewhere.

But I reckon the best ghost story we had back then was the story of Young Mister Spencer and the Family in the Attic.

Now, there are many kinds of ghost stories. Some you hear about when you're out camping and fall to spinning yarns around a campfire at night. These stories, though, generally ain't quite as scary, and so the teller has to rely on some accomplice jumpin' out from behind some tree or something right at the climax and startling everybody else half out of their minds. Another kind of ghost story just consists of one or two sentences:

"Did you hear Ol' Lady Simms got a ghost in her house? Yeah, it ain't much though. All it does is wander up and down the stairs all night making the boards creak."

But the story of Mister Spencer wasn't like no other ghost story. I can't really tell you why; it was just different. For one thing, even though we all knew the old Spencer place was haunted, none of us had ever been out there to verify the fact. It was like the haunting was part of the town's genetic makeup or something. Everybody knew about it, but few people knew the details. All anybody really knew for sure was that young Mister Spencer had locked his family up in his attic for years in the thirties and then killed them all off before killing himself, and as a result the whole house was as haunted as a graveyard.

Didn't nobody live in the old place; nobody'd ever really been in it since one of Spencer's people from Pennsylvania had come down to carry the bodies back up North. Town legend had it that this cousin or whatever tried to buy the place, but he spent one night there, left the next morning. and never did come back. Ever since then, though, the house had stood empty and overgrown (however, the chain gang did come out once every year or so and cut the yard).

Gardener first showed me the place one September afternoon back in '88 or '89 when we was playing hooky, me from school and him from the job he had gotten recently hauling wood for Mister Bellefield down off of Blevins Road. We needed to stay pretty much out aways so couldn't nobody find us and turn us in, and Gardener said he knew just the place, so we stowed my car back behind Parry's house, bought some burgers from Big Bob's diner, and took off in Bellefield's old dump truck.

I don't believe I have ever seen a house as large as the one Gardener wound up taking me to that afternoon; it 'bout most took my breath away. It had three floors, not counting the attic. A porch, which sat about six feet off the ground, wrapped around the whole thing. Each corner of the porch had this turret like construction, and the columns supporting the porch roof ran all the way down from the third floor. Every room on the second and third floors had its own balcony, and each balcony had two of these sculptured flower stands on either side, and even though they were mostly green and chipped from being out there so long, I knew they really had to be a sight when they had been new. The house literally dwarfed the old oak trees in the front yard, and the size of the yard itself (at least two acres), made it look like the house on top of the world.

"Hey Gardener. What the hell is this place?"

"Ain't you ever heard tell of Jacob Spencer?"

"Sure I have," I replied. "Who hasn't?"

"Well, this here's the place."

We walked around the yard for a bit, and Gardener jimmied the lock on the barn out back, but he would not go inside the main house.

"You can't go in there during the day, boy," he explained. "It ain't a lick of fun cause there ain't nothing in there no more. Besides, the folks round here are likely to call the police if they see us trying to break in. Just stay here in the barn and eat your lunch."

Gardener didn't say much more'n that, and I didn't press the issue, but I did wonder why the folks wouldn't call the cops on people breaking into the barn.

"You went out to the old Spencer place?" Parry was a little put out with us when Gardener dropped me off to pick up my car. He never said so in so many words, but I believe that he got his feelings hurt when we didn't ask him to skip out with us, but he forgot all about his disappointment when we told him where we'd gone. "What was it like? Did you go in?"

"Naw," I answered jerking my head toward Gardener. "He wouldn't let us. Kept babbling about folks calling the law on us."

Gardener didn't say nothing, but he glared at Parry when he started laughing.

"What happened, Gardener?" Parry teased. "Afraid Mister Spencer was gonna chop you in two?"

"Shut up, shitwit." Gardener suddenly turned all sullen and wouldn't look neither one of us in the eye. "I just didn't really feel like getting arrested while I was laying out of work. Is that so awful?"

"Oh, come on," Parry laughed. "You and I both know there ain't nobody that far out from town gonna call the cops on a coupla kids breaking into a house what's been standing empty for about fifty years and risk havin' them same cops find their stills or marijuana crops."

"Yeah, well," Gardener was getting real defensive now, "I just didn't want to take no chances. I mean I gotta keep my job."

"So by all means lay out on it Mr. Just-Don't-Want-to-Take-Chances. Come on, Gardener," Parry smiled at him, "you know what happened, and I know what happened. You were scared when you got there, and you didn't want to go in. There ain't no shame in it. Just admit it."

"You lookin' for a fat lip, pal? Cause I'll sure give it to you. I ain't afraid of a goddamned thing. I ain't afraid of no dead man, and I sure as hell ain't afraid of you." Gardener took a threatening step toward Parry before I could jump in between them.

"Hold on," I said, trying to push the two of them apart. "Both of you just cool down a little. This ain't no way to be."

"I'm just here to tell you," Gardener said, "I ain't afraid of nothing. Gardener Smith is not a chicken."

"Well, if you ain't afraid," Parry challenged, "I dare you to spend Friday night out there. You don't work on Saturdays, so I know you ain't gotta worry about gettin' caught playin' hooky."

"Hey, buddy, that's just fine with me." Gardener grinned right back at Parry. "But, ah ... You gonna have to stay out there, too. Else how you gonna know I done it?"

I swear Parry paled just a little when Gardener sprung that on him, but once he gave it a little thought he nodded and added. "Well, Gardener, I reckon you're right. But, ah ... we may need an objective witness, too. You know, somebody who ain't got nothing staked on either side of the argument to stay out there with us."

Gardener's smile got bigger, and both of'em looked straight at me like they was wolves what had just found a good sized rabbit for dinner.

"Hey, guys," I started shaking my head and backing away, "I can't; I got a date with Christy. I don't think she'll like it if I break it on her."

"That's all right, boy," Gardener put his arm around my shoulders. "I understand completely. You two can have one of the bedrooms all to yourselves."

Now, I didn't really think Christy would be all that agreeable to spending the night with me; haunted house aside, I'd only been dating Parry's cousin for about a month, and though I thought we'd been making pretty good progress in the making out department (my hand had just been allowed under the panties, and the bra was old hat by now), I still didn't think the all-night sleepover was really a concern for the near future.

"I'd love to go," she said. "Sounds like a heap of fun. I haven't ever been out there, and I love ghost stories. I'll just tell my parents I'm going off with Joanne, and we'll probably be late so we'll crash at her house. Pick me up after the football game by the field house, and we'll go from there. I'll get my brother to pick us up some alcohol. He does it for me all the time. Do you want me to bring you some, too? Or some food? No, we can grab some burgers on the way out there. That okay with you?"

"Uh ... sure."

If the house looked massive during the daytime, it was right forbidding at night. While you didn't really notice the cracked and peeling white paint, it positively glowed in the moonlight, giving the whole structure this eerie supernatural look. And the building itself towered over us standing at its base. It seemed to reach up and up and straight into the cosmos itself. Christy and I had gotten there a little late, and seeing Gardener and Parry's faint lantern light shining through the old ratty lace curtains didn't do much to lift the gloomy atmosphere from the place. If Christy hadn't've been with me, I don't mind telling you I don't know as Id've gone in at all.

But she was with me, so I did.

There was a little bit of furniture in the common room on the first floor, an old settee, a couple cushioned chairs, and an end table. I guess Gardener and Parry had taken the ancient dust covers off, 'cause I saw them all crumpled in the corner. The seats had been arranged in a sort of circle, and we found Parry and Gardener sitting on the settee passing a bottle back and forth between them. They musta been there a while 'cause neither one looked too sober.

"C'mon in, folks! We got the fire going real good." Gardener made a very broad and clumsy waving gesture with the bottle, spilling whiskey on Parry, who merely grimaced and stared at him.

Christy walked in and went straight for the proffered bottle. "Evenin', boys," she took a swig and handed it to me. "How's tricks?"

"Cain't complain," Gardener tittered, "Cain't complain at all."

I took the bottle (Southern Comfort it was) but only

pretended to swig; I didn't care too much for heavy drink, then; I generally drank beer. "So what's on the agenda tonight?" I looked at Parry.

"Well," he replied. "I believe we're all here to see just how brave Mr. Smith, there, is. So I figured we might ought to go on upstairs to see the scene of the crime, if you catch my drift."

Christy took another swig of Comfort and passed it back to Gardener. "What crime?" she asked. "I don't believe I've ever been told what the big deal about this Spencer is."

Parry stood up and patted her on her head. "All in good time, cuz, all in good time. Come on, Gardener. It's time."

As we started out to the foyer and stairwell, Christy nudged me in the ribs. "Hey, Loverboy," she whispered. "How 'bout taking some real swigs; we got a lot of catching up to do."

The attic was, not surprisingly, creepier than the rest of the house. Apart from the weird shadows the rafters cast from the lantern, the dust gave everything a pale and slightly distorted look. The three crude beds nailed to the floor in a sort of triangle on the far end of the room didn't help much, either. I took a "real swig" from the bottle and looked around for a place to sit.

Parry, however, walked straight to the beds and sat on the nearest one. Gardener took the one across from that, so Christy drug me over to the last one furthest from them but next to a window looking out upon the moonlit back yard.

"So you haven't heard about Spencer, huh?" Gardener flashed a devilish grin while he rolled this little cigarette. "Tell the lady, Parry. It's your show." With a flick of his wrist, he lit the cigarette and passed it to me with a wink. "Something to take the chill off your innards, boy."

"You see, Jacob Spencer moved out here back in the early twenties. He'd been over to Europe a couple of years before to take part in the Great War. Nobody knows what he saw over there, he never spoke much to the people around here, and his family was up in Pennsylvania or Maine or somewhere. Everybody just knew Mister Jacob Spencer came down with his wife, and bought this place from the bank, and was gonna try to be some kind of gentleman farmer or some such.

"Now after they had been here about a year, Jacob's wife, Natalie, had herself a pair of twins, a girl and a boy they named Grace and Samuel, and after that, Jacob and his wife began to emerge from their self-imposed exile and become part of the community. Didn't no two parents ever dote on their children more than Jacob and Natalie did, and didn't no husband ever worship his wife (or anybody else's wife, for that matter) more than Jacob did Natalie. You could see them every Saturday afternoon, his arm around her waist, she pushing a double stroller, as they walked up and down and all around the square. Passers-by would stop and coo and pet and pamper those two twins like they were God's own angels come to Earth. And Mister'n'Missus Spencer'd just grin. I swear, it was just like a picture on a Hallmark card. Jacob would spy other men eyeing his wife with a lust-filled gaze (preachers and politicians as well as drunkards, gamblers, and thugs), and he would just smile to himself in satisfaction.

"And they lived thattaway for about six or seven years when everything began to change." Parry stopped to take a drink from the bottle; I took another gulp and passed it over.

I'd done lost count of how many I'd had, I'd been paying so much attention to the story, but I was feeling all funny, you know, like you get, and it felt like I was watching everything through a glass of water somebody kept shaking up. I could hear the yard crickets chirping through the window at my side, and it sounded like music. Christy kept looking at me and smiling, and I got that sinking feeling in my stomach like if I wasn't too careful, something was gonna happen. Gardener was tittering about something sitting on his bed all crouched up with his head on his knees. I swear he looked like a little rodent there listening to the story and chittering to himself and smiling. I ain't too sure I like it.

Parry swam back into my vision, and I could just barely hear him over the music and Gardener's muttering.

"You see, when the Market crashed in '29, it hit everybody pretty hard. 'Specially down here where we had the boll weevil to worry about, too, and the Spencers weren't no exception. One night Jacob went to sleep in the house he owned all to himself; the next day he woke up in the house the bank owned. And there weren't a damned thing he could do about it. All the notes had been called in. All's he could do was walk into town and speak to the bank about when to get out.

"Well, my granddaddy, Lowell Caswell, he was the bank manager back then, and he says that he hadn't ever seen somebody as pitiful looking as Jacob Spencer when he came walking into that office that morning. 'That poor boy,' he told me, 'looked just like somebody had just pulled the earth out from under his feet like it was a rug, and he was falling and was gonna keep falling 'til Judgment Day. It about broke my heart to see him.'

"He come walking into Granddaddy's office and just stood in front of the desk with his hat in his hand.

"'I come to get evicted,' he said. 'The bank owns my house and my land, and I come to get evicted.'

"Well, you could'a knocked Granddaddy down with a feather. He'd never in his life had someone come in and ask to be evicted. He was so used to having to call the sheriff on evictees he didn't know what to do with Jacob, but he didn't really want to kick the man and his family out on the street.

"'Have a seat Jake,' he invited motioning towards a chair. 'Listen, there's no reason for you to be concerned. All this will pass, and everything will be like normal. Just calm down and ride it out like the rest of us.'

"'But I ain't got no money to pay my note. I can't afford to "just ride it out." Somebody's gotta bring in some money, or we'll lose the house.'

"'Well,' Granddaddy said, "don't you worry about it. You've always paid your bills, and we haven't ever had a lick of trouble from you. I'll tell you what: We don't have anybody banging our door down to try and buy the place right now. Why don't you all just sit tight and act as our caretakers on the place. An occupied house is a much better risk than an abandoned one. Stay there, and keep working the land. Try to get up the money if you can, but if nobody's tried to buy the place when all this trouble passes, maybe we can refinance. Is that all right with you?'

"Well, Jacob thought about it for a while, and I reckon he figured it was better than raising his family on the street. He took the deal and went back home. Now, like I said, things was tough all over. Jacob wrote to his family in Pennsylvania to borrow the money from them, but they were just as bad off. Seems they'd wrapped all their assets in the Market and wasn't a damned thing nobody could do. So he went back to farming what little he could and taking his surplus (if there ever was any) to town on Saturday, where didn't nobody buy anything anyhow, and he wound up taking it right back home again Saturday evenin'. When he walked through town, though, people still looked at his wife, and they still ogled his children, but Jacob didn't take as kindly to it no more. See, his wife didn't have any more pretty clothes to wear, and what she did have just hung on her like a scarecrow, and his children didn't look as healthy as they had done before. So Jacob figured the people were staring at them in pity or contempt, and Jacob had his pride. After a little while only Jacob came to town on Saturdays, and everybody figured he'd made his family stay home to protect them from the silent ridicule and abuse he felt the townspeople were staring to them."

Parry paused to take another swallow of Comfort and to let Gardener roll another cigarette. I looked out the window again. The wind had picked up a little outside, causing the trees to sway back and forth and cast improbable shadows in the moonlight. The crickets' music had taken a sinister turn, so I moved closer to Christy, who immediately snuggled closer to my shoulder. I saw Gardener, oddly backlit in the darkness, and he seemed to be humming along with the crickets and grinning like that weird looking cat in the Disney movie.

I wasn't sure what was going on, but the whole evening seemed to be turning weird. I took another drag off Gardener's cigarette, and Parry started again.

"Jacob kept getting more depressed and more sullen every week that went by and the depression didn't end. Every week that went by and the boll weevil didn't go away. By the end of the year, Jacob was just about the meanest and grumpiest man around. Nobody ever saw his family no more, and nobody ever spoke to him on Saturday afternoons unless they absolutely had to. But they all talked *about* him when he wasn't around.

"But Jacob kept on writing his family to ask for money, and they kept on not having any to give. Jacob kept on trying to grow his crops, and they kept on withering before they was ready to harvest. He kept on trying to sell what little extra he had, and people kept on passing his stand by. Eventually, he quit even bringing any produce out to his stand. He'd just sit there behind his empty bins and watch people pass by all Saturday long. I believe Jacob was losing his mind.

"Skunk Wilson'll tell you Jacob had locked his family in the house. He says he saw them one fall day about four years after Granddaddy struck his deal with Jacob and Skunk was cutting through the Spencers' yard to get to the creek back there and do some fishing. He was walking by when he thought he heard this tap-tapping coming from above his head. Well, he looked up and he couldn't see nothing since it was so bright outside, so he just kept on walking. While he was fishing, though, Skunk kept thinking about that tap-tapping. He couldn't concentrate on his line, he was so caught up in his thoughts, and he let about four or five fish get away from him.

"You know, tap-tapping don't just happen, he thought to

himself. No, sir, not this time of year. Woodpeckers don't come out much, and I don't know nothing else that tap-taps on windows, except people.

"So long about dusk, when Skunk figured he wasn't gonna get much fishing done, he decided to go back up to the house and figure out who was making all the racket. When he walked into the backyard, though, he turned white as a sheet. Staring right at him from out of the window in the attic was Samuel and Grace 'jest as thin as could be,' Skunk says. He says they were both looking down at him, and he swears they were begging him to come up and let them out, but just as Skunk was going to go in, Jacob turned into the driveway on his mule, and Skunk had to leave.

"However, he did go to the sheriff and tell him, and he did tell what he saw all around Owen. Everybody was curious about what was going on back in the Spencer house, but like the sheriff said, there wasn't any solid proof of anything illegal, so they couldn't really bother the man. When Jacob came to town the following Saturday, though (and every Saturday after that), everybody came to get a look at him to see if they could glean some kind of proof of what was going on up there. Jacob always said that his family was doing fine and thanked the folks for asking after them, but the old ladies and the drunkards all said they could tell by his look and manner that something was up, and nothing was good.

"Then about six months later, Skunk saw Natalie up in the window. Every since Skunk saw the children up there, he made it a point to walk by the house whenever he could, just to check, but he never did see them children again. One day though, he walked by, and even though he didn't expect to see anybody up there, he looked towards that window. She wasn't tapping on the glass or nothing; she was just staring out at the horizon with this lost and apathetic look in her eyes. But when she turned that gaze on him, Skunk's blood just about froze.

"'She looked just like a ghost,' he told me. 'She was all pale and her face was sunken in like even her bones had shrunk away. I knowed then, that Mister Spencer was gonna kill that woman. Just as sure as I'm standing here I knowed it. But wouldn't nobody listen to me. No, sir.'

"And that was the last anybody ever saw of Jacob Spencer and his family. Pass me that bottle, Christy, I'm parched."

"Well, what happened to them?" Christy asked as she passed the bottle over.

Parry waited to answer while he took a drink. "Don't nobody know for sure, really," he replied, "but Granddaddy says that a few days after Skunk started telling folks about Natalie in the attic, the bank received an offer on the Spencer property. When Granddaddy told Jacob about the offer, he didn't do nothing. Just stood there in front of Granddaddy's desk with his hat in his hands and looked at the floor. After a minute or two, he just turned around without a word and left the office. The next time Granddaddy heard from him was when he was called in by the sheriff to identify the bodies.

"'I knew that boy was upset,' he told me, 'but I sure never thought he'd go and do something this drastic. I still see those bodies, all bloated and disfigured, at night when I dream. Jacob couldn't be identified except by fingerprints; he'd blown his face clean off.'

"What must've happened was that Jacob came home after talking with Granddaddy, and he must've been powerfully upset. You see, a man needs his land. The land is what gives a fella his strength. It supports him just as well as he supports it. Jacob was strongly tied to that piece of land of his. He'd invested most of his adult life and all of his children's lives in that piece of dirt. He couldn't have known what to do without the land to support him. He had no place to go and didn't want to go there if he did. I imagine Jacob was completely tormented with the hopelessness of his situation. I'm sure he thought about his children forced to beg on the street for food and wife forced to do worse. I know he couldn't've found any of these prospects comforting.

"But this is all assuming he thought about anything. All we know is he killed his family in the attic. I don't know why they were up there; maybe Jacob had lost his mind long before my Granddaddy talked with him (there's certainly plenty of hearsay and circumstance to support that idea).

"He killed those people, though, just as sure as we're sitting here. He shot them in the attic, and then he turned that gun on himself. And Skunk found them three weeks later when he walked by the house to look in the attic window and smelled them from the yard."

"Well," Gardener interjected, "that ain't the way I heard it. I heard Natalie had been two-timing the poor bastard and that them kids wasn't his. I heard her lover confronted Jacob with the facts of the matter, and Jacob went back and strangled that other man's family with his own hands while they all slept. I also heard he didn't shoot himself; he hung himself from the barn out back." Gardener sat back with a self-satisfied grin, took another swig from the bottle, and passed it on to me.

"Well," Parry countered, "It don't matter. Who you gonna believe, somebody who was there or the town rumor mill? Everybody knows you can still here those kids and that woman whispering and crying at night. And everybody knows that Jacob still walks around in the attic like he's looking for his family and don't know where they are."

I took another swallow of Gardener's bottle, even though I knew I didn't really need anymore. The room had begun to spin slowly, first one way then the other in time with the crickets' music, and the lighting behind Gardener's head had become almost orange by now. Parry, though, seemed wrapped in a white light, an effect of the moonlight shining through the window behind him. Christy, who had fallen asleep on my shoulder, looked pale in the faint light. I shook her. but she wouldn't wake up for the longest time. "Come on, honey," I said. "It's time to go to bed."

She woke up just enough to stumble clumsily to the second floor bedrooms and fall asleep on one of the ancient musty beds there. She was still asleep when I brought up the sleeping bag and unzipped it to make a blanket. I crawled into bed next to her and slowly tried to undo her shirt from behind, but she grabbed my hand and held it to her chest, emitting a satisfied snore as I laid next to her trying to fall asleep. I guess I knew nothing would happen tonight.

The moonlight streams through lace curtains and an autumn breeze blows through the open window. Though the air should be fairly comfortable, I have caught a chill. I sit up and rise from the bed to close the window. The cold has come early this year, and I don't want her to catch her death of pneumonia. As I close the window, I turn towards the bed, but she isn't there. I don't know where she could have gone. I don't remember her leaving.

I walk over to stoke the fire, but the embers are cold. The air is cold; I am cold. Everything has gone cold. Cold came early this year. I pull on my clothes and leave the room. The boys will be downstairs sleeping near the furnace. Maybe she has gone to join them. I open the door and descend the stairs.

The house is as dark as death at this time of night or morning or whatever the hell it is. Dark and cold. As I enter the common room I hear voices whispering and chattering in the corner.

"Shhh. Listen there Gardener. He's walking. Do you hear it? He's walking the house!!"

"Can't you shut the fuck up for one damned minute? There ain't nobody up, but Christy or her gentleman caller, and they may be up, but I guaran-damn-tee you they ain't walking around up there. Now shut up and let me sleep."

"I'm telling you; he's up and he's walking the house."

She's not down here, though. I don't know where she is. Maybe she just had to go to the bathroom, and she's back in bed now. Yeah, that's probably it. She just had to go; she did drink a lot, and it all has to go somewhere. I ascend the stairs again and return to my bed.

I see a female form in the bed and watch her chest rise and fall in steady breaths. Rise ... fall. Rise ... fall. I crawl back into bed and curl up next to her, but her skin is cold to the touch. I try to sleep. Nothing will happen tonight. They are all safe.

The noises won't stop though. Haunting music seeps through the walls. I know it's the crickets; they've been chirping like that for almost as long as can remember. At night, though, it's enough to drive a man crazy. I know it's crickets, but it sounds like a fiddle. Maybe some damn fool actually is playing the fiddle. Damned hobo camp out in the woods. Sheriff ought to run them bindle stiffs out, but he won't.

Over the fiddle though, I hear something else. A quiet, high-pitched sound from upstairs. Those kids playing more jokes, most likely. I try to ignore it, but once you notice a sound like that, it just gets louder and more intrusive. I reckon I'll have to go shut them up. With a sigh, I rise from the bed and put my clothes back on.

"Hear that, Gardener? It's Natalie crying. He's walking the house, and she's crying. I told you."

The voices are coming from downstairs, but I still hear the high pitched sound from the attic. It rises and falls in an almost rhythmic pattern. I open the door to the attic, and she sits on the bed looking out the window.

"We buried them out there," she said. "First the girl, then the boy." She points out the window. "Right out there. Under their tire swing. I didn't want to let them go, but it had to be done. We didn't think they could endure that much more pain."

As I draw nearer, she turns around to look at me. Natalie Spencer is one of the most beautiful women I have ever seen; she always had been. Sure she's not as sensual as Emily Blanchard, and she's not as well put together as Christy Davis, but she has a different kind of beauty. She wasn't born with her beauty; she earned it. Earned it by moving across the country with her husband and leaving her family. Earned it by giving birth to a pair of precious twins who were too weak to live past thirteen. Earned it by burying her children while she herself was young. Natalie Spencer was more beautiful than anyone because she had *earned it.*

"You couldn't finish the job. After you dropped the first spade of dirt over their tiny bodies, you just collapsed. I had to finish and carry you back."

As I near her, I see the pockmarks and scars on her face. She coughs once and tries to smile. "We didn't know it stayed in the room. We didn't know it carried in their clothes. We couldn't afford the doctor, and we didn't know how serious it was until we saw that Grace had gotten it, too, and Samuel wasn't getting any better."

Gardener crouches in the corner grinning and giggling, red-orange glow behind him. He doesn't say anything, though, just grins. Parry stands in the opposite corner bathed in moonlight; he doesn't do anything, just watches quietly.

"I couldn't bear to see them suffer so. It broke my heart. Their little bodies were being torn up, and we couldn't make them better. You made it as painless as you could for them, and when you had finished, you tried to carry them outside, but I wouldn't let you. I had to be the one. I brought them into the world, and by God, I'd be the one to take them away from it.

"After they'd been gone a week, though, I couldn't stand it, so you brought them back and put them up here. When I caught it, I came to live with them, but I don't think I can stand it anymore. It hurts."

Gardener whispers, "Do it." I see the children lying on the beds as if they were asleep. Natalie coughs and cries at the same time. Scratch plays a fiddle in the distance. Somewhere a bell tolls.

"It hurts."

"Do it."

"It hurts."

"Things ain't always what they seem," Parry whispers.

"Do it."

Parry turns away.

I place the pillow carefully over her face and lay her back in

*the bed, pressing gently but firmly. After a short while, she coughs
again and lays still. I remove the pillow and kiss her good-bye.*

*The soil is hard to break, frozen solid. Cold came early this
year. I do it, though, and I place the family in the shallow pit.
Mother first children at her bosom. I do not collapse after the first
spade of dirt. I finish the job and mark the place. Ashes to ashes.
As I return to the house, I admire the structure. It looks like the
house on top of the world, and I am proud.*

*In the common room, I find a piece of paper and my service
revolver. Two lines: "They're under the tree. Fix them right."*

*Parry, in the corner looks sad. "Things ain't always what they
seem," he says.*

Gardener opposite him just grins: "Do it."

Sunlight woke me late the next morning. I could hear
Christy say something and Gardener laughing downstairs.
Parry said something else that made them laugh again. When I
went down, though, Parry and Gardener got all sheepish and
went out to pack their cars. Christy came over and gave me a
kiss.

"We didn't think you were ever gonna wake up, Loverboy.
You sleep like the dead."

I kissed her back. "What were y'all laughing about down
here?"

"Gardener thought it was funny when I said that you acted
like the perfect gentleman last night and didn't try nothing.
Then Parry told me about hearing all those noises last night
and how Gardener couldn't hardly sleep at all, he was so
nervous."

"Oh." I replied. "Well, things ain't always what they seem."
But I wasn't sure which statement I was responding to. I picked
up my bags Christy had packed for me, and we walked out the
door into the yard. I locked the place up before we left.

Interlude

I know what people say about me. They think I'm a little odd. They spread rumors about me. I see the way adults turn their heads and get all quiet when I'm around. Oh, they'll speak to me, tell me "hey" and ask about my day. But they don't really want to know about me. Their ideas and rumors are so much more interesting than the truth, they think.

The children, too, have their ideas and names and legends about me. I hear them at school and in town when they think I can't.

"That man is crazy," they say. "He stays cooped up in his house all the time except to buy food and go to work. I heard tell he spent time in Milledgeville."

"Fool, Milledgeville ain't had a nuthatch for years. Not since my daddy was little."

"Well, he's about as old as your daddy, maybe he went when he was little."

I'm thirty-one, but don't let the facts get in the way of a good story.

Once you all hear my story and take me back, nobody in town will be surprised. They'll hear the truth, add to it to make it interesting, then shake their heads and cluck their tongues.

"I always knew that boy'd come to a bad end."

"And a shame, too. Why his best friend used to be none other than Gardener Smith, himself. I don't know where he could've gone wrong."

They'll pretend to be shocked, but they'll secretly be pleased. They'll have someone else to look down on. After a week, maybe two, there'll be something else to gossip about. The facts and reasons won't matter. Only the event itself, shrouded in myth and supposition, will have any importance.

Later, when the furor has died down and just punishment exacted, the town will find another scapegoat, someone else to pity, scorn, and fear, and I will have been forgotten by all except the children.

For the children, I will become the stuff of legend, and fireside horror stories.

"And then the crazy janitor threw the sack full of body parts into the lake in the woods, and he was never heard from again." The voice grows quieter as the speaker leans in closer to the flames. "Except, every once in a while, he can be heard scrambling in the woods, looking. Looking for another victim."

At this point a confederate hiding until now will jump out from behind a tree, scream, and throw a bag over one of the listeners' heads.

I will be the stuff of legends.

V. The Primrose Path

So Emily didn't hardly ever talk to me no more. I never did know exactly why; she just slowly withdrew into her own world: waitressing at Hell's Ditch and sleeping in the shack out in the woods. I didn't really notice it at first, I was just a kid, you know. I lacked about six months of graduating high school and nearly four months after that of being eighteen. Emily Blanchard, like many friends over the years, had begun to quietly slip into my background so that I hadn't spoken two words to her in three months before I ever realized that we weren't speaking. It bugged me, but once you notice something like that, suddenly all those weeks of silence come rushing at you and you see just how long a time it's really been and you know with every fiber of your being that you just can't go up to that shack and knock on the door and say, "Hey there, Emily. How you been keepin'?" After such a long time, it's just easier to worry yourself (and anybody you are still talking to) about it than it is to actually do something.

"Hell, boy," Gardener counseled, with that damned old Gardener shit-eating grin he had, "that girl's doin' just fine. She's workin' regular, and she's got some extra money comin' in. She ain't got time here lately for shit like a social life. She gets plenty of sociallin' from her work. Leave her alone; she knows how to find you if she feels like talkin'."

I asked him where her "extra money" was "comin' in" from, and he grinned that grin for a while and told me he sent her work from time to time, but he wouldn't elaborate on what kind of work. "Good payin' work," was all I could get out of him, but I figured it was right considerate of Gardener to look after her like that, and I thanked him for his concern.

"Believe me, boy," he said, "It is my pleasure. I'll tell her you said hey."

So I let it slide some more. Gardener was taking care of her and as long as she was alright I was satisfied. Like I said, I had a lot of other stuff to worry about. I was a senior in high school and damned near eighteen, and while it seemed every other guy in school was making shotgun wedding plans or quietly trying to raise money to get themselves "out of trouble," I still hadn't been able to coax a girl to my bed. I'd been seeing Christy for nearly six months and still couldn't get past third base. Parry kept telling me I had to be patient and take it slow, but after four months of this advice, I became increasingly convinced that he was concerned more with preserving his cousin's virtue than assisting his best friend's right to rite of passage.

"Look," he finally advised me one afternoon, "do I look like Dr. Ruth? I don't know what the hell to tell you. Furthermore, I don't think I'm really the one you need to be having this conversation with. If I'd've known it was going to be this damned complicated, I'd never have gotten involved. Talk with Christy; she's the one you want to sleep with. Just leave me out of it. Please."

Christy wasn't quite as understanding as I had hoped when I tried to explain a man's needs to her during our next date.

"Look pal," she said, "I've got myself to think of. I sure as hell don't want a kid right now and seems like that's all that stuff leads to. There's more to life than gettin' married right out of high school; I don't care how many folks're doin' it. And I sure as hell ain't gonna risk all that for some guy who ain't even in love with me."

Well, this just flew all over me. "Who said I ain't?" I demanded.

"I did, that's who. Look, you're a real sweet boy, and I love goin' out with you, but I know just as sure as my name's Christy Davis that you ain't no more in love with me than Parry is. Oh, you like me, no doubt about that, but you don't love me. And I won't go further than I have gone for anything less."

"Maybe I do love you," I returned, but really just to get in the last word.

"No," she shook her head. "It ain't me you love. Now, come on we're gonna be late for the movie."

Christy didn't think I loved her, and until she did, I'd never get any further with her than I already had done. I wasn't real sure if I loved her, either, and I didn't have the foggiest clue how I could convince her if I did. So I figured I may as well just get used to the idea of spending the rest of my life a virgin, but, as usual, Gardener stopped me.

"Look, you do love her, don't you?"

"I don't know," I replied. "Maybe ... I think."

"Well hell, boy. That's close enough. If you think you love her, you may as well. Actually lovin' 'em's not the problem. Girl's like that, all you gotta do is make'em think you love'em, and shoot, that's just as easy as fallin' off a log, son."

Now, I know Parry'd told me time and again how I shouldn't ought to listen to anything Gardener said. That he'd lead me straight down the primrose path to hell if I gave him just half a chance. I knew Parry was right, too. But everything Gardener told me made perfect sense. It had to be true, and the truth couldn't get me into trouble. If I didn't love Christy, as long as she thought I did, she couldn't get hurt. Besides, I did like her, and if I tried hard enough, I just might realize I loved her, too. Either way, I was young and these were things everybody had to go through in order to grow up right.

"It's called the maturin' process," Gardener declared solemnly, "and can't nobody reach adulthood until they've gone through it."

All the same, I didn't tell Parry about Gardener's advice. He did say for me to leave him out of it.

I started calling Christy for no reason at all. This would show her that I couldn't do nothing but think about her all the time.

"I was just sitting here thinking about you," I'd say, "and I thought I'd call you up and see what you were up to."

"Nothing much," she'd reply. "Just watching *Cheers*, but there's a commercial on right this minute [she loved that show; I think she had a crush on that Ted Danson guy, but she never admitted to it]. What're you up to?"

"Nothing much," I'd answer her back. "Just thinking about you. That's all."

"Well, if there's nothing you need, I reckon I'll let you go, the commercial's over."

"Don't hang up," I'd plead (and this was my master stroke), "I'll turn it on, too, and we can watch together."

"You're a freak," she'd reply with a sarcastic coyness, but she wouldn't hang up, and I knew I had her hooked. See? Gardener knew what he was talking about.

In addition to calling her all the time, I wrote her notes all day long in class. She'd be waiting in the hall when I got out, and I'd give them to her. She'd smile and look down when I did. Then she'd hand me a note, too. It was always filled with how cute I looked today. How much she missed me during the last class and how she couldn't wait 'til we went out on Friday night. I began to think that maybe I was in love with her because these notes made me feel all warm inside, and I started looking as much forward to her notes as she looked forward to mine.

Love poems were the next step. I'd write her one a day, every day. And I gotta tell you, she really ate those up. I made them rhyme and everything; man, I was good! She didn't write me any poems, though. I don't guess she was all that talented that way.

Everything was going exactly like I wanted it to.

Finally, I knew Christy knew I loved her. It happened one Friday just before last period. I had outdone myself that day. I called the florist and had half a dozen pink carnations sent to her during lunch. I even wrote my best poem ever:

If I were a rich man,
I'd buy you the Taj Mahal

79

(I'd buy the Seven Wonders
If that would help at all)
I'd crawl across the desert
Or walk barefoot over coals.
I'd suffer slings and arrows
[We'd just read Hamlet the week before];
I'd give to you my soul.
But I don't got much money
So there ain't much I can do
'Cept give you these flowers
And say that I love you.

And I had it stuck into that green Styrofoam stuff with all the flowers. Man oh man, did she ever love that!

When I was walking to my last class that day, I saw her walking straight for me. She had this look on her face like she was real intent on getting to me before I went into class, so I stopped and waited for her. Well, when she got up to me, she smiled real big, grabbed me by both shoulders, and kissed me right on the lips like we were out on a date and couldn't nobody see us. Took me completely off guard (just between you and me, I had to take a minute to adjust my books in front of me before I could go into the room). When she was done, she looks at me all serious like, and says:

"There's more where that come from, Loverboy. Don't be late tonight."

Well, I swore right then and there that I'd never doubt Gardener's words again.

It took me awhile to settle on just the right kind of condom. I mean I hadn't ever really given much thought to it before, but my Daddy told me time and again that it was the little things in life that counted the most, and I sure didn't want anything to mess up this evening. So after about twenty minutes of diligently studying the family planning counter of the local Revco, I finally settled on Big Buddy's Brand Ultra-Thin, Super-

Sensitive, Maxi-Lubricated, Mega-Spermicidal condoms (ribbed for her pleasure) from the men's room in back.

Next, I stopped by Sothesby's 24 Hour Car Wash and Pool Hall where I washed and waxed my primer grey '79 Honda Civic. I vacuumed the interior and let the back seat down to enlarge the hatchback area. I wanted to create just the right atmosphere, so I paid the extra seventy-five cents for the Caribbean Holiday Pina Colada scented spray. I threw in some extra towels for good measure.

Finally, I went home, took a shower, brushed my teeth (being sure to spray more than my usual dose of Binaca down my throat), and put on my best pair of jeans. I didn't button the top two buttons on my shirt, preferring to let my gold chain show through my thinly haired (but by no means bald) chest. Besides, that'd be two less buttons to undo later. I opted for loafers due to *their* ease of removal as well. My denim jacket slung casually over my shoulder, and I was ready to go when the phone rang and Christy told me she couldn't go out on account of her parents needing her to watch her kid sister.

About ten o'clock, with nothing better to do, I decided to go visit Emily at work and found myself at Hell's Ditch eating one of Bob Crumb's world famous Grease Burger Supremes and half-heartedly picking at a wilted chef's salad with ranch dressing and crumbled captain's wafers for croutons. Emily, though, wasn't nowhere to be found. I had to settle for Big Bertha instead, but that was okay, I reckon, since I never really had to order when Bertha waited on me. She always just met me at the counter with a burger, a salad, and a reasonably passable glass of ice tea.

"Come on down here, son," she said when I walked in. "One booth with food. No waiting." Then, when I sat down she ruffled my hair. "I'd give you a deal on tonight's special," she said as I tried to lay my hair back down flat, "but I know you ain't int'risted in nobody but that 'ere girl o' yourn."

I got to admit, when Bertha talked that way to me while

mothering me like she did, it made me feel all weird inside, but I swear I couldn't tell if it was revulsion or not. So I generally ignored these remarks.

"Where is that girl tonight, anyway?" she asked when she came back to fill up my glass and clear away my empty dishes.

"Her daddy wouldn't let her go out tonight," I explained between bites. "Had to babysit her little sister or something."

"Boy, what's wrong with you?" Bertha made a big show of feeling my head like I was burning up or something. "Unless Emily's moved out of that shack out there, she ain't got no father to keep her home. All I know is she ain't been to work in 'bout a week, and I figured she was takin' a few days off to cool down a little, but ain't nobody heard hide nor hair of her since her accident. Is she alright or ain't she?"

"I don't know," I replied. "I didn't know nothing about it."

"'Didn't know nothin' about it?'" she glared at me. "I thought you two were tight. What about Gardener? Didn't he say nothing? He's the one came and got her..."

"Bertha!!" Bob yelled over her. "Quit that gabbin' and pick up these orders!" He wiped a dollop of sweat of his forehead without regard for the chili he was standing over and scowled through his unlit cigar butt. "You got customers to take care of with us runnin' short-handed."

Bertha walked off to take care of the other tables, muttering at Bob the whole way. I knew I'd wait for her to come back, though; I didn't have nothing better to do, and I sure as hell wasn't gonna leave 'til I'd heard what this "accident" that Gardener didn't tell me about was. She came back around about fifteen or twenty minutes later with a slice of pecan pie. She set the dessert in front of me, handed me a fork, and told me the rest of the story.

It was Bob that found her. He'd told her to go back to the kitchen and slice up tomatoes, and when she'd been back there for over twenty minutes and her customers were complaining too much, he went back to see what the hold-up was.

"Bertha!!" he yelled out. "Bring me a mop and call the ambulance."

When Bertha got to the kitchen and saw what had happened, she almost fainted.

"I'm a tough woman," she looked embarrassed, "you pretty much have to be in this business, but I ain't never been able to stand the sight of blood. And, honey, I hadn't ever seen that much blood. I'd been after Bob to fix or replace that damn slicer for months, and it took this to get him to do it. That girl sliced both her arms so bad I didn't think we'd ever get the bleedin' to stop."

Gardener had been visiting Emily before she went to the kitchen, and he went back there to help, too.

"Ain't no need callin' no ambulance," he said. "They'll take forever, and she's liable to be dead before they get here." Then he took off his t-shirt, ripped it in half, and made two bandages. He used masking tape to try and hold them over the wounds, but that wouldn't do no good. He grabbed a couple of rolls of paper towels and shoved them up under her armpits and made Bob squeeze her arms tight around them. Then he took off his shoes and unlaced them, using the strings to tie his bandages to the cuts. By this time the bleeding had slowed up some, so he asked Emily to squeeze her hands into fists. When she did this, Gardener smiled despite the fresh streams of blood that squirted out the wounds.

"I don't think she cut any tendons," he announced. "I'll go ahead and take her to the hospital myself."

Bob expressed concern over workman's comp (specifically his not having any for his employees) and wanted to make sure Emily realized she'd had only herself to blame for not taking correct safety measures. Gardener then reminded him that Emily, herself, had been in violation of the law for working underage when she was hired. Then he added as he helped Emily out (making sure her hands were raised) that he was sure something could be worked out and not to worry, that he would, he said, "take care of everything."

Well, you better believe that once I heard this, I went straight out to the shack to see how Emily was doing, and I don't mind telling you, I felt a little disappointed by both her and Gardener. I mean I thought we were all as tight as Bertha thought we were, and there wasn't no call in keeping me in the dark like that. So, yeah, I was going to check on Emily, but she was going to get a piece of my mind in the process, too.

I kept telling myself this as I got out of my car and strode into the woods towards the shack keeping the creek on my left and bearing right at the lightning tree. Over and over again, both of 'em were going to get a piece, and they better get to explaining pretty quick. By the time I reached the clearing, I'd worked myself into quite a lather. I stomped onto the porch with such a fury that I scared myself with the loudness of my steps in the quiet night. Then, once I recovered myself, I rapped as forcefully as I could on the door.

"Emily!" I yelled. "Gardener! Open this goddamned door before I break it down!"

No answer except for the sound of some animal, deer or something, running off from behind the shack somewhere into the woods.

"Emily!! I ain't even kidding! Open up!"

Still no answer.

"Awright, then," I continued, "if you're gonna be that way..."

Something fell over inside. I turned the knob. Unlocked.

"Emily?" I wasn't yelling no more as I stepped inside. The front room was creepy, what with no electricity and it being about the middle of the night, but I noticed a faint crack of light coming out from under the door to the back room. "Emily? You alright?"

Silence. I stumbled over a pile clothes and kicked something little and plastic across the floor and fumbled my way to the door to the back room. It was locked when I tried the knob.

"Emily, you in there? It's me. I just came by to check on you. Bertha told me about what happened. Open up this door now."

When she didn't answer, I slammed myself into the door as hard as I could, but it wouldn't open. I tried again and heard the dead bolt start to give away from the other side. On the third try the door gave way with a deafening clap against the wall a lot faster than I thought it would. I fell flat on my face and slid across the floor about a foot until I hit an overturned chair.

I raised up on my knees, rubbed all the floor dirt and dust bunnies off my face, and looked up just in time for a bare foot to catch me under the chin. I had found Emily.

The rope hadn't been tied right or something. She was dangling there about two feet off the floor kicking to beat all Hell and grabbing frantically at her throat to loosen the knot, but the only sound was the creaking of the rafter she'd lashed herself to as it strained under her weight. She just kept dangling and kicking and scrambling at her neck but not making any noise, like a silent movie almost. Even in the faint candle light from the corner, I could see that she was turning blue, and her eyes were all bulging like they were going to pop right out. I don't even know if she knew I was there.

"Emily! What the Sam Hell're you doin'?!" I scrambled to my feet and started looking frantically for something to cut her down with. My stomach started with the sinking feeling again, worse than ever, and I couldn't get my feet to work right. All I could do was scurry around helplessly and gibber and stammer and blather like Bob Newhart on acid.

"Oh, Jesus," I kept saying. "Oh my God! Oh my God! Oh my God!"

The creaking got louder and that just set me off worse.

"Where the hell is a knife, Emily? I know you got one." Like she was going to stop what she was doing and answer me or something. "What do I do? What do I do?"

I was panicked now and stopped where I was, crying like a baby.

"Jesus H. Motherfucking Christ won't somebody tell me what the hell I'm supposed to do???"

Then, as if in answer, the rafter split half in two, and Emily crashed to the floor, gasping. Without the weight on the rope, the knot had loosened a little so she could breathe.

"You didn't tie it right," I informed her to break the ice (and prove that I wasn't scared) after we had calmed down and I finished loosening the knot around her neck. "It's supposed to loop around thirteen times, and you only did it twice. Also, you didn't jump from high enough. Jump higher up and the rope snaps the neck. The way you did it just would have choked you to death."

She looked at me funny, then broke into a coughing fit. "No shit?" she replied when she got herself under control. "I'll remember that next time. What're you the Angel of Death or somethin'? Just untie the damn thing and leave me alone. I don't know what the hell you're doin' here, but I'd appreciate a little privacy."

"Well," I got all defensive, "I came by to check on you. Bertha told me about your accident."

Emily gave a hollow laugh. "Accident. Is that what they're callin' it? This look like a accident to you?" She stood up and thrust her arms at me, and I saw that Bertha wasn't quite correct: Emily was cut further down than her arms. I tried not to give away how uncomfortable I felt looking at them.

"What is that?" I asked, struggling to keep my voice even. "Fishing line? What kind of doctor'd you go to?"

"Didn't go to no doctor." she replied. "Cain't afford it if I wanted one. Gardener did this." She smiled at me but only with her mouth. "You know Gardener. Just full of hidden talents."

"What's wrong with you, Emily? Why didn't you and Gardener tell me about any of this? I would've helped you out; you know that."

She glared at me in that way she had that made me feel ashamed of myself for no good reason. "Would you have?" She asked. "I just bet you would, and you'd want just what ever'body else wants, too. No thank you. I got plenty of 'friends' willin' to help a girl down on her luck. 'Sides, you ain't been in no terrible hurry to help me, lately. It's been months since you graced my doorstep. What's so different about my life that you decided to grace it tonight?"

I couldn't think of nothing to say. This reunion was almost exactly like I figured it would be. I knew I'd been away for a long time. Emily and I had grown further and further apart, seeing each other less and less every week that went by since she started working at Hell's Ditch. Yeah, I should've come sooner, but, like I said, it was just easier once the habit of staying away had grown. I couldn't think of no reply to Emily's accusations, so I just sat there, dumb.

"So what do you want now, buddy boy? What do you want?"

I looked up at her. I ain't sure if it was sweat or something, but my cheeks felt hot and wet. My lips were salty. I didn't say anything, though. She was standing over me, thrusting her fishing line wrists in my face. Forcing me to look at them.

"What do you want?!" She was yelling at me now. Crying really. "I ain't got nothing left for you! I'd give you my blood, but I cain't even do that right. So tell me, Mr. Angel of Death, just what the hell do you want from me?"

I couldn't take any more of this. I didn't want to look at her wrists anymore, so I knocked them away. I stood up, kicked the rope across the floor, and walked out of the room.

"That's it, boy," she hollered after me. "Run away. That's all you're good for, runnin' away."

In the front room, again, I stumbled over the same pile of clothes and kicked another little plastic cylinder and a spoon. Bending down, I also saw a light scattering of white dust on the floor around the pile. I picked up the plastic cylinder and just stood there staring at it intently. I don't know what I was looking for in it. Answers? Hope? If I was, I didn't get none of it. It was just a needle.

"Is that what you want?" Emily had come to the door and was watching me. "Take it," she said. "Gardener brought me plenty." She laughed her hollow chuckle again, "It's good for what ails you."

I turned to look at her silhouetted in the doorway, scarecrow thin in shadow. I was sweating something awful but only on my face. I couldn't speak much above a whisper or my voice would crack. "Emily," I muttered, "why do you hate life so much?"

She was silent for a long time before she answered. "It's all I can do," she said. "It ain't never brought me nothing but misery. No momma, a daddy who don't love me right. I ain't got nothing going for me."

"You got a house over your head," I returned. "A steady job."

"I live in a fallin' down slave shack," she was really crying now, "and I ain't much better than a two bit whore workin' for food and smack. Some life."

"Excuse me?" I said, but I knew it was true. All of it.

"I'm a sixteen-year-old prostitute junky." She wasn't yelling anymore. "I sleep with men for money and food. I give the money to Gardener for the junk, and he sets me up with the dates." She looked at me, eyes gleaming in the dim light. "If I don't do it, Gardener'll tell Daddy where I am. At least here, I get paid for it." She slid down the door frame and pulled her knees up to her chin. "Now," she continued, "you tell me why I hate life. You tell me what I got to be thankful for."

I didn't talk for a long time; I couldn't think of anything to say. I thought about everything she had said...

Gardener and his smug grin and creepy wink. "She ain't got time here lately for a social life," Gardener told me. "She gets plenty of sociallin' from her work." I bet. I remembered Gardener talking about how he'd "take care of everything" and "send her a little side work from time to time." I thought about how many times he told me she owed him money and how many times I'd seen him walking out of the woods counting it.

"How much she owe you?"

"Enough," he'd say with a guarded look.

Emily and the needle. Always sleeping or groggy. Humming dreamy children's songs as she rocked slowly back and forth on the porch. I remembered her bathing in the lake two years ago. She looked just like any other fourteen-year-old girl. I remembered how she could live at my place 'til she was thirty-three and I wouldn't never try nothing. J.B. on her lighter.

"My perverted asshole of a father," she said.

I remembered Big Bob Crumb, "Emily, get your ass out here if you want to keep workin'! Do that shit on your own time!"

"How's work?" I used to ask her.

She always gave a hollow chuckle. "Fine," she'd reply. "Regular."

How could I have been so blind?

"Well?" she interrupted my thoughts. "You gonna talk or what?"

"It ain't me you love." Christy said.

"You ain't int'risted in nobody but that 'ere girl o'yourn," Bertha teased me.

"Did you hear me?" Emily interrupted again. "What do I have to live for?"

"Me," I said quietly. "I think … I think I love you."

"You think so, huh?" She looked at me funny, then away. "Who told you to think that?"

I walked over to her shadow in the doorway. I was beginning to feel all funny inside again. But this time, it was okay. I put my arm around her. She didn't move away, but she didn't lean into it.

"Nobody," I replied quietly. "I just do."

She didn't look at me when I said this, and I had to strain to hear her next words.

"You don't know what love is," she whispered. "You don't know shit about shit. How could you?"

I closed the door as we went into the back room.

Emily didn't say nothing as she took off her shirt. I couldn't hardly see much in the pale candle light, but I could tell she was a lot thinner than she was the last time I saw her. Her breasts were pale, and I could almost see her ribs. But I was too nervous to care really. She still didn't look at me directly, and this bothered me a little. I figured, though, it was on account of her being so preoccupied with loosening the button on her jeans.

When she got her jeans off, I was a little surprised to see she didn't wear no underwear. I could see dark veins running up and down her arms and legs, and vague dots appeared around the inside of her elbows when the light hit them just right. Then she stood straight and faced me like she was trying to meet my approval or something. I just stood there staring at her pale body, her chafed neck, her tired eyes. I smiled timidly.

She moved closer and put her hands behind my head, and none of that mattered, not her paleness, not the shadows under her eyes, not nothing. She looked at me and smiled just like that Mona Lisa painting. I wondered, briefly, if she was happy.

After Emily kissed me, I was so discombobulated I couldn't even unbutton my shirt right. I popped two buttons before she pulled my hands away and finished it herself. I thought I was going to die. With every button she loosened, she'd kiss my chest and give it a little lick.

Since she was better at it than I was, I let her help me off with my jeans, too. I did feel a little silly there for a minute when I was standing with my pants and shorts around my ankles wondering what the hell I was supposed to do. I felt all wiggly inside when I looked down at her and saw her spine hunched over my feet. I wanted to sit down on her mattress, but my legs wouldn't let me. She never spoke.

I watched her slowly rise to her knees and take me into her mouth. I ran my fingers through her hair as her head slowly bobbed back and forth, back and forth. Her mouth was warm and moist; the room smelled like musk scented Speed Stick. I could feel her tongue wrapping all around me as she gave it a little suck. I didn't care about nothing then except how good it felt to be standing right where I was: above a girl on her knees, my hand in her hair. Back and forth, back and forth. Her tongue all around me. Back and forth, back and forth. I'll just be honest with you; I'm surprised (and a little proud) that I didn't just explode right then and there.

She pushed me back on the mattress; I kicked my shoes off. The left one hung a little and distracted me. I kicked at it again, but it wouldn't come loose. I tried to pry it off with my other foot. She was straddling my knees and beginning to crawl towards me. The shoe still wouldn't come off no matter how hard I pushed. She reached my head and began kissing me again. I imagined I could taste myself on her breath, but the image lasted only a second as the shoe finally popped off my foot, flew into the air, and landed on her back.

She finally led me into her, but she still kept squirming on me, though she did move a lot slower now. I decided to try to knock the shoe off by throwing all my weight one way and getting a little more reach with my arm. I think she misunderstood my intentions, though, 'cause she moved with me and we flipped over. The shoe fell off her back, slid off her mattress, and landed somewhere on the floor as I found myself laying over her with no more distractions. I pushed myself up on my hands for better leverage and thrust into her as far as I could.

I felt as if I was plunging into an abyss: I could feel the sinking feeling in my stomach start to rise, and it felt good. Thrust. I felt warm and wet all over my body. I wanted to go deeper. She moved her legs over my shoulders and mumbled something I couldn't understand. Thrust. Her arms reached up and her hands wrapped around my back. I felt something lightly scratching my sides. Thrust. She began to knead my lower back, but I still felt the scratching on my sides. A little rougher now.

Her fingernails began running up and down my spine, and the scratching moved further onto my back. I couldn't even pretend to ignore it now. My movements became mechanical, but she didn't seem to notice. She kept her eyes closed and continued to rub my back. I could no longer feel anything except the scratching. I didn't want to stop and find out what it was, but I couldn't really concentrate on anything else. This was worse than the shoe. It felt like a whole bunch of staples. Short and stiff.

I vaguely noticed her quicken her pace and hold me tighter. The scratching felt like it was just under her hands a little. She pulled me faster. Harder. Short and stiff. More like the twisty-tie things you put on garbage bags than like staples. Faster. Scratch. Harder. Scratch.

I moaned aloud, shuddered, and fell on my side away from her. I realized what it was.

We laid there for a little while not saying nothing. I felt empty inside, like I had lost something. I mean I enjoyed it, no doubt about that, but I didn't feel much different when it was over. Emily was so thin and pale, I felt, later, like I hadn't done nothing but hump a skeleton. I wasn't too sure how I felt about my first sexual experience: in a rundown shack out in the woods with Emily's stitches on my back.

I looked over at where she was laying all huddled up on her side of the mattress. I could tell she'd pulled her knees up to her chin again and wrapped her arms around them. I realized she hadn't said a word throughout the whole experience.

"Emily?" I touched her shoulder. "You okay?"

She moved away from my hand.

"Emily?"

"Thirteen, huh?" she said quietly. "I should have cut down instead of across."

I put on my clothes a little bit after that. I don't know if Emily was asleep or not; she didn't move when I got up. I tried to buckle my pants quietly in case she was. I pulled on my right loafer and made a half-hearted and fruitless search in the dark (the candle had just about sputtered out by now) for the left one but gave it up when it didn't leap right out at me. I'd get it later.

As I pulled my shirt over my shoulders, I looked down at her form on the mattress. She still had her back to me, and while her knees were still tucked under her chin, she had pulled the blanket up a little to cover her bare shoulders. I could see them move when she breathed, though, so I knew she wasn't dead or nothing. I figured she was all right, now, and I could go back home.

I ain't sure why I couldn't stay there. I mean, Dad didn't care whether or not I came home on weekends or nothing. He'd just figure I'd crashed over at Parry's or something and forgot to call. So I *could* stay, but I didn't feel right doing it. It seemed like the longer I stayed on that mattress with Emily, the more I felt like something the cat drug in. I couldn't figure it out, but I felt like I should have been ashamed for the way I done her and staying any longer in that shack just made me feel worse.

So I buttoned what was left of my shirt and left.

The sun was just starting to think about rising when I go to my car. I reached into my jeans pocket for the keys, but they weren't there. I tried the other pocket. Nothing.

"Shit." I saw them dangling from the ignition. The door was locked. So were the passenger side and the hatchback.

"Hey, boy, looks like you could use some help." Gardener scared the bejesus out of me. I turned around, and he was standing right there looking over my shoulder into the car. "You ain't got your keys, huh?" He grinned the stupid grin again. "Don't worry," he said. "I'll take care of everything."

"Like you been helping Emily?" I asked. "No thanks. I've seen enough of your helping."

"Boy, what in the Sam Hell are you talkin' about? I ain't been nothing but supportive of that girl."

"Don't fucking lie to me!" I yelled at him. "You been using her from the get go! She told me all about it, Gardener! And I'm here to tell you, Mr. Smith, it's gonna stop today. I don't want you around that girl no more."

Gardener just smiled bigger, like he was gonna laugh. "You don't, huh? Well, I gotta ask you, boy. How you gonna stop me?" He looked pointedly at the missing buttons on my shirt and my bare left foot. He smiled again. "You think she's free, now? How she gonna support herself? You gonna provide for her?" He ruffled my hair like a parent. I squeezed my hand into a fist. "That's cute, boy. It really is, but Emily's right, you know. You really don't know shit about shit. Now you run along home and remember your first lay and let other people get on with their lives. She's been around enough to know what's..."

I punched the shit out of him and couldn't believe it. Right on the side of his head. It whipped around like somebody jerked real hard with a string. When he got himself under control again, though, he looked at me real hard, but I didn't bat an eye.

"Leave her alone," I said. "That's all I got to say."

He rubbed his cheek and didn't say nothing for a while. Then he bent down and picked up an old tree limb, and I damn near shit myself.

"Well," he looked into my car and back at me. "We'll see about it." Then he swung the limb back as far as he could and let fly. I couldn't help it. I ducked as it crashed into my window and shattered it.

"In the meanwhile," Gardener continued calmly, "you look like you could use some sleep. Drive on home, boy. I told you I'd take care of everything." And he walked away as if didn't nothing happen.

Now, I know I should've told Christy about what had happened. I should have told her right off, but I didn't know how to tell her without hurting her feelings, so I figured I'd wait 'til Monday at school. Maybe I could think of something to say over the rest of the weekend.

And if I couldn't, she'd be much less likely to kill me in front of four hundred and fifty students and faculty.

I should have told her as soon as possible; I know and understand this now. As it turned out, though, Gardener found her before I did.

"You're a pig," she seethed at me when she found me during lunch (I'd been able to avoid her up to then). Christy had this way of gritting her teeth real hard when she was angry and trying not to yell. It was worse than any yelling she could have done because the effect was like somebody had turned her volume down. So not only was I getting reamed up one side and down the other, but I had to actually strain to hear what she said. "I have never been so insulted, degraded, and hurt in my life."

"Christy, let me explain... "

"Shut up." She put both her fists on her hips and stared me down like I was some kind of criminal or something. "You don't have any right to explain a damned thing. I trusted you. I believed you at least cared for my feelings if you didn't care for *me*. But you don't care for nobody but your own self."

"But, Christy, you're wrong I... "

"What? You do care? Bullshit. I had to hear about you and Emily from *Gardener Smith* of all people." When she said Gardener's name she twirled her head around, causing her blonde ponytail to swish in a way that was inappropriately attractive. "You didn't even have the balls to tell me yourself, you had to send a messenger."

"But I didn't send Gardener, I... "

"So you were just not going to tell me then?" There was, apparently, no way I was gonna get a word in edgewise. "Gardener took it on himself to tell me?"

"Yes ... No ... I mean... "

"Oh, quit it. You didn't even care enough to let me know. Admit it. You don't give a shit."

"But I do!" I finally got a word out. "I do care. I care about your feelings."

"You have a wonderful way of showing it."

"I care about Emily. I think I even love her."

"Oh, now that's choice. You love her? Last week you loved me. Which is it?"

I knew that no answer I could give would help my case much, so I shut up.

"Which is it? Huh? If you really cared about Emily, you wouldn't have done that in the first place. You wanted to get laid; that's all. And congratulations, buddy boy, you did. I sincerely hope you feel proud of taking advantage of a poor, fucked-up girl like that." While she talked, her hands waved all around, but when she finished, it was like she didn't know what in the world to do with them so they just kind of hung limp there in the air. I got to admit, though, I was more'n a little afraid she'd decide to hit me with them.

"I didn't take advantage. I..." I had to defend myself now, but she wouldn't let me.

"Yes you did. Don't be dumb as well as blind, boy. I know all about that poor girl, the whole town does. Do you really think she wanted to have sex with you? Did she say so?"

"No, but... "

"But you got all hot and bothered and decided she was easy pickings. I bet you never once thought of her, did you?"

How good it felt to be standing right where I was, above a girl on her knees, my hand in her hair.

"Did you?"

Plunging into an abyss, sinking feeling in my stomach starting to rise, and it felt good.

"Say something."

But I couldn't. I knew she was right, and I couldn't defend myself against that.

"Don't fucking talk to me, again." The bell rang, and she turned sharply on her heels and marched off to fifth period.

After that, Christy didn't hardly ever talk to me no more.

VI. Home I'll Never Be

Nobody was really all that surprised when Skunk Wilson passed. He was, after all, close to a hundred, according to his best guess. See, birth records weren't ever all that kept up back then, and Ol' Skunk, well, he had to do the best he could with what all he remembered. He knew he'd been about fifteen when Halley's Comet came in 1910, so he just counted up from there. He'd lived in Owen his entire life; his family had belonged to the O'Neals before The War of Northern Aggression (as Dad called it, The Civil War to everybody else). After Lincoln freed the slaves and the war ended, Skunk's folks wanted both to leave their past lives behind and yet didn't want to stray too far from the familiar, so they took the name of the O'Neals' nearest neighbor, the Wilsons, and they kept working for the O'Neals. When Old Man O'Neal started the new cotton mill, the Wilsons moved into the mill village and started working there.

"Seems like workin' for O'Neal was just a habit," Skunk used to tell us. "Like pickin' your nose or bitin' your toenails. You don't never understand why you do it; you just do."

When Skunk was old enough, he went to the mill, too, and he worked there just about every day of his adult life until the Depression hit, and the mill closed for a while.

Afterwards, though, when the mill started up again, during the war, Skunk just couldn't seem to make himself go back.

"I'd done broke the habit," he explained. "I reckoned it was easier to break that one than to quit pickin' my nose and bitin' my toenails."

And as far as anybody ever knew, Skunk Wilson moved into the back alley behind Reno Phillip's pharmacy and didn't never hit a lick at a snake all the rest of his days.

So when, on the morning of March the 18th, 1989, he didn't come out to the front of the store like usual and sit on the bench there with Enos McDougal, nobody was surprised to find that he'd "gone on to a better place." The town did mourn, though.

Skunk Wilson was, after all, pretty much a fixture in our little town. The oldest man in Owen, the only first generation freeman anybody ever knew, and the best firsthand knowledge of our town around. When Skunk died, so did the greatest archive of Owen's history (I understand that even that rat bastard, Gardener Smith, got misty eyed at the news, but tried to cover it up by blaming his tears on the combination of dust, heat, and the thought of how ripe Skunk must've been when they found him that afternoon). We were all grieving, but wasn't nobody surprised at his death.

His wealth, though, shocked the shit out of every man, woman, and child for miles around.

Like I said, nobody'd ever seen Skunk do an honest day's work since the mill closed down. Oh, he'd occasionally sweep the streets for liquor money, and usually the next day he'd pick up litter in the park for public drunkenness. But as far as steady work with a salary and benefits (or even just a salary), if Skunk Wilson had one of them, none of us ever saw it.

So when his last earthly remains were prepared for the memorial service, we were all a little surprised to hear that none other than Claude McRory, the most prestigious mortician in three counties, was fixing him up rather than the county man in the morgue. More than a few eyebrows were raised when we learned that he wouldn't be laid to rest at The First Christ Fellowship in God's Holiness Church out in the county on Blevins Road just past the Blanchard place.

"It'll be the Perpetual Peace Park, for sure, then," Parry said to me when he heard about it. "I reckon that's the only other place he could possibly be put. Maybe, when he helped them clear out that land a couple or three years ago, they just gave him one of the plots they never could sell over there close to the swampland."

None of this, though, compared with the absolute bewilderment with which we met the next development of

Skunk's funeral.

"Engraved invitations?" Parry called me up on the phone as soon as he got his. "Hand-delivered, no less."

It was true; Enos McDougal's grandson Billy had got himself all dressed up and delivered each invitation to just about every household in town. Dad had gotten his and handed it on over to me. "I suppose," he said, "we ought to go see this."

I looked at the invitation:

The family of the late
Ulysses S. Grant Wilson
respectfully request your attendance
at his memorial service.
His Second Coming Mausoleum
Saturday, March 23, 1989
10:00 AM

"Ulysses S. Grant?" I asked.

"Forget that," Parry countered, "The *mausoleum*? You got any idea how much that costs?"

"10:00 *AM*?" Dad added from across the table. "On a Saturday?"

I was amazed to see how many of Owen's citizens turned up for Skunk's funeral. There must've been a thousand or so. Like me and Parry, I figured most had come just out of curiosity, to see what other surprises Skunk had planned. Since there wasn't no way we were getting Dad's butt out of bed on a Saturday morning ("not even if Reagan, himself, keeled over dead"), me and Parry left nearly half an hour early for the services. His Second Coming Mausoleum sat way in the back of Our Lady of Perpetual Tears Memorial Garden, but by the time we drove up, there were cars parked all over the cemetery (even on a few of the older, less well-known graves). So many folks had shown up, the funeral director had erected a speaker system outside the mausoleum itself, and his assistant was busy handing out folded funeral home chairs and blankets for the overflow to sit on.

"I reckon we better get in line for a chair or something," Parry said as we worked our way through the crowd towards the door. "It don't look like we got too much of a chance at getting inside."

I nodded absently as I spied Enos all dressed up in a tuxedo ushering some folks into the building and turning others away. I was just about to turn towards the funeral director's assistant when he called out to us.

"You boys need to hurry on in." he said as we came up to him. "Mr. Wilson wanted you here especially." He put a hand on each of our shoulders and guided us into the building before closing the mausoleum doors. "You all just go and find your places. It's about to start."

There wasn't any room in the back rows, so Parry and I had just about decided to stand in the back when we saw Enos again. He was up near the front shaking his head at us and pointing to three empty seats on the second row. Well, we felt a little presumptuous sitting all the way up front like that, but he kept on pointing, so we slowly made our way up there. Sure enough, both our names and Gardener Smith's were taped to the back of the chairs.

"Now sit down, boys," Enos said. "Here they come."

No sooner had we sat down than a hush fell over the congregation, and the doors at the back of the mausoleum opened. There was no sound at all for a few seconds except for the slow, steady footsteps of the pallbearers as their heels clicked in unison on the marble tile. Then, as we all turned our heads to see the procession, the front and rear pallbearers began to sing a round:

> *Jesus, we never knew who you was*
> *Jesus, we never knew who you was*
> *You was borned in manger*
> *But died the king for us.*

I lost track of the rest of the song once I got a good look at the casket. I ain't talking about no pine wood box with a little polish on it. This thing was huge. It was gold all over with silver trim and the sunlight through the windows reflected off it so much it almost hurt your eyes to look at it. I couldn't help myself, though. It took eight people in full tux and tails to carry it. Every time they took a step to the beat of their song, I was afraid the damned thing was gonna tip over and spill old Skunk out on the floor! Truth be known, I kinda hoped it would so I could see what they'd dressed him up like. I was also curious as to what else they'd crammed in there; this box was huge. And it had trim on it like a Cadillac, I ain't kidding. It even had a hood ornament that looked like an angel speeding its way to the afterlife. It looked just like something out of a Robin Leach special.

After they carried Skunk and his golden crate to the front and set him up on a little stand, Brother Robert Cray led us in a prayer and introduced the speakers. The list of speakers was no less surprising than the rest of the service. Judge Taylor spoke for about twenty minutes followed by the Mayor, a few alderman, and a representative from the state legislature. Apparently, over the years Skunk Wilson had invested in homeless shelters all over the state and donated bundles to various local charities, and everybody had something to say about his "Christian virtue and humility."

The biggest surprise of all, though, came when Brother Robert introduced the final eulogist. Robert was known far and wide as a long winded speaker. He was the kind of person who, if given a choice between explaining something in ten words or fifty, he'd figure out a way to say it in a hundred. When he got up to introduce the last speaker, though, he just kind of said the name and sat down without another word as Mr. King, the high school English teacher and local murderer, took the podium.

Edwin Paul King never had a chance. His daddy was the

meanest man ever to take a breath of air, and everybody knew it. You see, Latham King had a thing for the bottle. He spent every waking moment either shit-faced or rapidly on his way to it, and when he got there, he got violent. Latham beat that boy of his from sun up to sundown nearly every day of his formative years. When he tired of the poor entertainment Edwin offered, he'd take on the more satisfying sport his wife Jackie provided. With Jackie, Latham could not only beat her senseless, day after day, but he had the added pleasure of bodily humiliating her while his boy was powerless to do anything about it.

Nobody knows why Latham beat his family; they certainly never gave him cause. Maybe he was angry that life hadn't turned out the way he'd imagined it. It's got to be galling to have a name like King and live in a tarpaper shack with debt up to your hairline. Maybe he felt inadequate as a provider for his family and their faces, day after day, only reminded him of his own shortcomings. Or maybe he was a direct line descendant of Cain and family violence just came as naturally to him as eating and sleeping came to most other folks. Regardless, the town knew him and his family and what he was like, but that didn't stop them from shunning young Edwin, when he shot the old bastard through his temple with his own .38.

And we were no different. How often had we sat there in his classroom while he droned on and on about Oedipus, Hamlet, and Willy Loman, nobody paying attention to a word the man said and making no secret of it. We knew and he knew that he was powerless. All his classes were the same: by the second week of school, Mr. King had given up on motivating us, and we, in return, had given up any pretense of respect for the man. So he merely gave the same lecture over and over again, changing only the relevant character names:

"Things aren't always what they seem," he leaned on his desk and rubbed his glasses on his shirttails. He had the thickest damn glasses I had ever seen, and when he placed 'em back on his face, it looked like his eyes took up the whole of both lenses. I don't think there was a thing he could see. He strode up and down the rows of desks talking to the air. "In fact, they almost never are. Isn't that what this play is about? Everything Oedipus believes is incorrect. It isn't what it seems. His mother is his wife, his children are his siblings, and the plague is his fault. Nothing is as it, at first, appears.

"While this is, indeed, an important theme in *Oedipus Rex*, though, there are other, perhaps more important, themes in the play. Themes that, together with these differences between appearances and reality, make this play far more than simply an exercise in awareness. Can anybody tell me what some of these other themes are?"

He paused and looked around at the class. Parry was asleep in the back corner. Robert Dunn aimed a rubber band at Gilbert Evans, the preacher's boy, and didn't stop when he saw Mr. King looking at him. I tried to pay attention, I really did, but everybody in school had heard some version of this lecture at least once a year. In fact, Gilbert was the only one in the classroom taking notes.

"Anyone at all?"

Finally, when it became obvious that even Gilbert wasn't going to offer up anything, I raised my hand. "Responsibility?" Almost all his lectures eventually made it to this theme, and I figured that by going ahead and skipping to it, I might shorten the lesson and put everyone out of their misery.

"Very good," he smiled at me, but I turned away. "What does this play tell us about responsibility?"

I'd given him his cue; I'd be damned if I contribute any more. I stared forward. Robert got me off the hook. He let his rubber band go at Gilbert's ear with a "whack" followed instantly by Gilbert's girlish shriek.

"Responsibility, Mr. Dunn, is taking credit for one's own works. Wouldn't you agree?" Mr. King had made his way to Robert's desk and took up his arsenal of rubber bands. "This play tells us that we each should take responsibility for our own actions, good or bad. The gods don't care about extenuating circumstances. Other people don't care about extenuating circumstances. The only people that really care about extenuating circumstances are the people committing the offenses.

"Does Oedipus have extenuating circumstances? Sure he does. He has the best excuse available. He honestly didn't know. He truly meant no harm. The only crime he consciously committed was the sin of pride. He felt he could change what the gods had decreed for him, and as a result, his people suffered. His family suffered. He suffered. He didn't know his circumstances, but... "

The bell rang, and we left Mr. King with Oedipus' suffering.

We knew Robert would never get in trouble over the rubber band. Mr. King's position at the school was treacherous at best: an acknowledged father-killer teaching literature and grammar in a small Southern town don't got a lot of job security. He wouldn't risk Robert telling his folks about it. Who would they believe? A known liar and juvenile delinquent or a murderer?

"If I did tell Dad about it," Robert reasoned. "He wouldn't do nothin'. Ain't nobody in town gonna take that killer's side. Who's gonna listen to somebody that not only shot his daddy in cold blood for no good reason, but has been 'unnaturally close' with his mother ever since? No, I ain't got nothing to fear from that pervert."

As for Gilbert, the preacher's son, he'd just chalk it up to God's righteous fury for not taking part in the class discussion and let it go at that.

While we all knew what Mr. King had done, very few of us knew many of the details. There were all sorts of stories and rumors floating around about what had happened. Some said Latham caught Edwin and his mother in some kind of compromising position. He took the boy out "for a ride" and a fight ensued in the car during which a gun went off. Others said it was the other way around, that Edwin caught Latham with Jackie, but nobody really doubted that incest was somehow involved, the King's being from "that part of the county."

The more charitable of the townspeople usually allowed for Latham's affinity for the bottle and domestic abuse.

"Now, you boys got to learn to see the world from other folks's point of view," Skunk Wilson told me and Parry once. "Take that Mr. Edwin y'all is always whisperin' and snickerin' about."

"What about him?"

"Well, in all your whisperin' and snickerin' did it ever occur to either of you that maybe you didn't have all the story? You all tease that poor man and call him all sorts o'names behind his back, but do you know anything about him?"

"Like what?"

"Like, for instance, Ol' Mr. Latham used to beat that man every day of his life from the time he could walk 'til he was about y'all's age and Latham had his accident. When he wasn't beatin' on his boy he was beatin' on his wife. Now you boys imagine the life Mr. Edwin had to live. What would you a'done?"

Sheriff Bentley, too, seemed charitable towards Mr. King. "You all will hear a lot of big talk from folks with little information and smaller minds. First of all, there wasn't no fight 'tween Edwin and Latham at their house. Latham got drunk one night, took Edwin out for a spin, and wrapped his car around a tree out past Dock Waller Road. The whole town knows that Latham King was one mean son of a bitch. If you could see the bruises Jackie used to have, and I don't know how many times Edwin had his arm or leg in a cast. I don't care what folks say happened. Latham King died from injuries sustained in a car accident. That's what I put on my report, and that's what happened.

"As far as this talk about Edwin and his mother," Bentley continued after a pause, "I don't know a thing about that, and what's more, I don't want to know."

All I knew about Edwin outside of school was that he generally just kept to himself. He and his mother had moved into the town after he came home from college. They bought themselves a little two bedroom house about a block from the school, and Edwin walked to work every morning, and if he had any shopping, he'd walk the three blocks to the Quality Foods Super-Thrifty Mart.

He would not buy a car.

Nobody ever saw them much unless somebody ran into them at the store (but even then, they wouldn't speak to them). They did not receive visitors. Clive Hendricks, the mail man, left their mail on the porch. Other than Clive, I didn't believe anybody else ever set foot on the Kings' property.

And so he stood there, watching us watching him. He took off his glasses and began to wipe them with a handkerchief. We waited patiently; his former students in the audience had to've known a lecture was coming. Finally he replaced his glasses, poured himself some water from the pitcher beside him, and held both sides of the podium while staring out over the audience.

"Ulysses S. Grant Wilson," he said, emphasizing each syllable, "was a great man. I don't believe anybody sitting in this room today truly realizes what a great man the man in that casket was. I don't mean to say that you didn't like him. I'm sure you all did, but you never understood him. Mr. Wilson was the most generous man in Owen, and nobody ever knew it except him, the bank, and one or two others. Name any park in town or any other public work and you can bet that Mr. Wilson had something to do with it. Mr. Wilson was a man who truly cared for everyone. He never had time for a family until it was too late, so Owen became his family.

"Ulysses S. Grant Wilson was misunderstood because you couldn't look beyond his appearance and see what he really was. All you saw was just another homeless nigger living in a cardboard box behind the pharmacy, and as long as you saw that, you never understood the man. He could have bought and sold each of you three times, but he chose instead to care about you more than you cared about him.

"I understood him because I have lived his life, too. When my father passed, none of you ever tried to understand me. You saw me only in the simplest terms: a patricide, father-killer. You never asked me what happened; you figured you knew. Poor son of a drunkard shot his daddy in cold blood. The least charitable of you said more; the most charitable said less. No one, though, bothered to ask me. You simply put me aside in your righteous fury and ignored me. Only Mr. Wilson bothered to understand me.

"Ulysses S. Grant Wilson made me the man I am today, and for that I am forever grateful. If Owen was Skunk's family, Momma and I became his favorite children because we looked past his appearance and loved him for who he was. He was the only person to visit Momma and me after the accident and see that we were okay. He hired a lawyer for me who had all charges quietly dropped, and he continued to provide for us throughout the years. I owe my job to the man in the casket. I owe my house, too."

As he spoke I heard several folks shuffling in their seats and even a couple of "uh-huhs" and "I told you so's" under people's breaths. I couldn't help but wonder why Mr. King was telling all this to us now.

"I'm not deaf. I heard and continue to hear the stories, lies, and gossip people tell about me. I remember after the accident, when I wanted to explain my side of the story, Mr. Wilson told me not to.

"'You'll just give them more reason to gossip, son,' he told me. "They ain't gonna listen; they'll just take the juicy bits and twist'em to fit their own ideas. Don't make it harder on yourself and your mother.'

"So I never said a word. For three decades I have kept my mouth shut. Mr. Wilson and I made Momma stay home so she wouldn't hear the awful things you say about her. I do all the errands for her. And for the last thirty years, Mr. Wilson has come once or twice a week to sit and visit with her. When he sent me to college, he cared for Momma while I was away. When I came back, he'd take nothing from me other than my appreciation for his help. Mr. Wilson was the best father anybody could have had, and I stand before you today to tell you what a father you missed."

"I have also come for another reason. Mr. Wilson came to our house last week.

"'Eddy,' he said to me. 'I ain't never asked you for a thing you're entire life. I felt right sorry for the childhood the Lord give you, and I was happy to make your and your mother's life better than it had been. I never wanted anything in return, but I want to ask for something now.'

"Of course I told him I'd be happy to do anything I could for him.

"'I ain't got much longer to be here,' he continued, 'I reckon the good Lord's fixin' to call me on home soon. Now, I done made all my arrangements for afterwards except one. Eddy, I'd be much obliged if you'd speak to the people at my funeral.'

"I told him I'd be honored to deliver his eulogy.

"'I want you to tell them people about what happened to you. I reckon I told you wrong all them years ago when I said to keep quiet about the truth, and it's growin' on my conscience. A fellow has a right to try and be understood. Them people got to learn one way or the other that things ain't always what they seem, and you got to take responsibility for your own actions. Ain't that what you been teachin' the young'uns all these years? So you promise to tell'em what's what and put my mind to rest.'

"And so, that's exactly what I'm going to do."

He took a long drink of water, and then he began.

My Dad could be the meanest man in the county when he drank, and I don't think anybody here would deny it. He beat Momma. He beat me. He even beat the dogs. Sometimes he'd get drunk in town and try to beat other folks, too (even the police officers as they carried him off to the drunk tanks). When he was drunk, I hated my father with every fiber of my being. I knew with a certainty bordering on the religious that one of these days he'd throw that one punch too many and somebody was gonna shoot him the head. To my shame, I sometimes hoped it would be me.

When Dad was sober, though, things were different. He was my Dad, and I could love him. He'd take me fishing or hunting. He had my first fish mounted when I was five. It was a little brim about three inches long, but he had that fish mounted and he hung over the fireplace in our cabin right there next to his prize-winning bass. He kept every picture I ever drew in kindergarten folded up and wrapped in plastic in the bottom of his bedside table in a drawer all their own. When he was sober, I loved my Dad more than anything else in the world.

When I was fifteen, he tried to teach me to drive a car.

He'd been drinking earlier that morning, but he hadn't hit me or Momma yet, and I figured he was okay. Besides, it was ten o'clock at night, and I hadn't actually seen him take a drink all afternoon. So I grabbed my jacket, and we left. The lesson started well; he only sighed loudly when I had trouble coordinating the gas and the clutch.

"You have to develop a feel for the pedals," he said. "You'll get better."

But after a while, the constant stalling out of the engine began to wear on his nerves. "You're not listening to me, dammit. Just like always. Let the clutch and the gas out evenly! I keep tellin' you that, what the hell's your problem?" He stared out the windshield. "And for Christ's sake quit getting nervous, or I'll give you something to be nervous about!"

After about thirty minutes of this, I began to get fed up with it. I mean there's only so much a person can take. "Dad," I said, "if you don't shut the hell up, I swear I'm gonna pull over and you can either drive yourself or walk home."

Now I knew this wasn't the best way to handle a belligerent drunk, but I felt I'd run out of options; ignoring him hardly ever worked. Of course, this tactic didn't work much either I found out as his fist slammed against my ear.

"If you think you're man enough to kick me out of my own car, *boy*, you just go ahead and try. I brung you into this world, and I'll sure as hell take you out. And I'll tell this, too, I wouldn't miss your sorry ass either. I'd just make another look just like you."

I tried to go back to ignoring him. *Concentrate on the road*, I told myself. *This is not the time or the place for this kind of nonsense. Keep your mind on what's going on.*

"You hear me, sonny boy? What? You gonna cry now, like a girl? I always thought you had more of your mother in you than you did me."

Just ignore him and get the car home. Keep your mind and your eyes on the road. It's dark and winding, and you don't want to get lost. But he wouldn't let up, not for a minute.

"That it? You a girl? I bet you squat to pee. Do you squat to pee, girly?"

Even out the pressure between the gas and the clutch. Do it slowly, just like he said.

"Godddammit, Edwin! Quit poppin' the fuckin' clutch before I pop you, too!" He lunged over the armrest and grabbed at the wheel. "Gimme that sonabitchin' thing; I'll take us home so you can go cry in your room."

I shouldn't have done it, but I wasn't thinking. As soon as Dad's hands started grabbing at the wheel, I punched him as hard as I could in his face, and once I started punching, I couldn't make myself stop.

"You ungrateful son of a bitch!" he screamed, and I could smell the sickeningly sweet smell of his whiskey breath, "I'll learn you to hit me!" And he bit me right on the arm as hard as he could. Hard enough to draw blood.

I screamed and completely forgot about the car, the road, the clutch, and the gas. All I thought was *This is it. I ain't taking any more crap from this drunk bastard.* And I laid into him upside the head and face like it was the last day that face punching was gonna be legal. And I just kept yelling and crying over and over each time I hit him.

"You will not hit me anymore! You will not hit mother, anymore! *You're* the worthless piece of shit! Don't ever fucking hit us again!"

I don't know how fast the car was going when it ran off the road and down the embankment, but it was almost too fast for the tree to stop it.

A buzzing in my head woke me up. It wasn't constant, though; it was a series of short buzzes like an intercom, but they were too long and quick to be an intercom. Then I heard Dad's voice behind it.

"Eddy? Eddy? You awake, son?" Maybe it was my alarm clock.

It sounded like the night crickets out by the road. Then I remembered and slowly opened my eyes.

"Eddy? You okay?" There was something about his voice that wasn't right.

"Yeah, Dad, I'm fine, I think. Just a little bruised is all. How about you?"

"I'm okay I reckon; I feel a little numb in places, but I'll manage." His voice was sobered up now, but it was also muffled a little, like he was far away. He must have busted my eardrum when he hit me. I'm sure the crash didn't help much, either.

"Listen to me, son. Don't move if you can help it. I heard a few cars a while back, I'm sure they'll send somebody out for us directly. The main thing is for us to sit tight 'til they get here. It won't be long."

I looked over at him, but he wasn't in the passenger seat. There wasn't really a passenger seat; it had disappeared along with the door. In fact, nearly the whole car was just a crumpled piece of metal. Dad wasn't anywhere.

"Dad?" I asked. "Where are you?"

No answer. Some dogs howled out in the woods.

"Dad?"

"I think the tree threw me out of the car. I'm out here somewhere. Sit tight, son, I'm sure somebody's coming for us."

After about two hours, I got tired of waiting. I'd heard about six cars drive by but nobody stopped, so I figured they probably couldn't see us from the street. My legs were sore, and my back hurt, but I felt okay otherwise. With a little work, the door opened enough for me to crawl out.

Once I gained my feet, I started looking around for Dad. The headlights were casting weird shadows all over the place, and it was hard to make out much. The tree had smashed through just about all of the passenger side of the car. What it hadn't smashed had folded up under the car like a banana peel. The car had done its damage, too, though. The top half of the tree, a good ten feet, had snapped off from the impact and lay about three yards away. I couldn't see Dad anywhere.

"Dad," I called, "I'm going up to the street. I don't think they can see us."

His voice came from the other side of the fallen tree. "Come here."

I looked under the driver seat for a flashlight, but I only found Dad's pistol. I grabbed it and checked behind the seat. His toolbox had, of course flown open in the wreck and I had to dig and sort through all kinds of tools and stuff before I found it. The batteries were weak, but they'd do.

Dad was pinned under the tree a couple of yards away from the car.

"Try to lift this thing," he said, "I'll go with you."

"Dad, I don't think I ought to do that. What if..."

"Dammit, son, lift the tree. I can't feel my legs!" I reached under, but I couldn't lift it much higher than a few inches before it fell out of my hands and landed back on his leg with a disturbing crack. He let out a scream, and then fell silent, breathing heavily.

"I'm sorry, Dad, it's just too heavy for me by myself."

I turned the flashlight's feeble beam to the tree. Dad's legs were more than pinned. They looked as flat as Wile E. Coyote after the Roadrunner took a steamroller to him. It was going to take nothing less than a tractor to move this tree.

"It's okay, son," Dad weakly patted on my foot. "You tried. Better go onto town before it gets much later. Leave that gun with me in case those dogs get curious."

"I gave him the gun and the flashlight, and I left my jacket with him in case he got cold before I returned.

"Be careful, Eddy. I love you."

I said nothing as I climbed the embankment and started for town.

I walked for about an hour before Jasper Bellefield passed me in his dump truck heading out of town hauling wood. He said he'd drop me off back at the wreck to keep an eye on Dad, and he'd head into town for help.

"Why don't we head on into town now?" I asked. I was oddly anxious to get help for Dad.

"We're closer to the wreck than we are to town and someone ought to let the man know help is on the way." So he brought me back to the embankment. "Don't worry, kid," he said, "I'll be back as soon as I can." He waved as he turned his truck around and headed back into town.

Dad didn't answer when I told him what was going on as I slid down the bank to the car. I figured he'd dozed off while I was gone. All I could hear was the chirping of the crickets and popping as the engine cooled. Even the dogs had quit barking. I looked over at the tree and saw the faint glow of the flashlight as its batteries continued to dwindle. I called for him again and still received no answer.

When I reached the tree, I realized why Dad wasn't answering. He was breathing shallow, his eyes were squeezed shut, and he was gritting his teeth. He kept making little squeaking sounds like a dog whimper.

"Mr. Bellefield's going to bring us some help," I told him, but it was clear he couldn't pay me any attention. That's when I noticed the blood pooling at his head. "Daddy?" I said softly, "What'd you do?"

He just clamped his eyes tighter and the whimpering became a long, low moaning.

I didn't really do anything; I simply took the gun from his hand and sat staring at it and him for a long time. I didn't think about the times he beat us. I didn't think about the times he yelled. I didn't think about the good times or the bad times.

All I could think about was the time he ran over the cat's back legs. We'd been about to go to the store when the cat ran out in front of the car. I remember him getting out and looking down at the thing vainly clawing the ground with its two good front paws and mewling quietly.

"Only thing to do," he said, "is put it out of its misery."

When Jasper returned with an ambulance and Deputy Bentley, they found me sitting and staring at my father. I sat and stared as they took the gun out of my hand and put me in the ambulance. While they examined me and released me from the hospital, I sat and stared. I sat and stared when Mr. Wilson bailed me out and when the lawyer got the charges dropped. In a way, I have sat and stared for thirty years. He didn't reckon anybody'd want to believe the real story once I told him what happened. We figured if we ignored it, it would go away. But it hasn't gone away. Only Mr. Wilson has.

Nobody said a word as Edwin Paul King stepped down from the podium and walked out the door.

As Perry and I left the funeral that afternoon, I couldn't help wondering why Skunk wanted us there. I mean I would've come anyway, even if it had been at Perpetual Peace or even The First Christ Fellowship in God's Holiness. I always liked him. He never missed a chance to talk to us when we'd come by the pharmacy and pester him (even Enos would eventually get irritated with us and bitch and moan until he moved to another bench).

Seems like he was always trying to get me to look past people's appearances.

"Things ain't always what they seem," he'd say. And, boy, was he right. Who'd've thought that all those years ago he'd bought all that stock in the cotton mill and waited for the next war and its inevitable demand for textiles. Who'd've thought that all those years he'd been living off a pittance while he saved most of his money and sold land he'd bought with the rest. Who'd've thought that he'd support a poor white trash family and put the son through college.

Then I thought about Edwin King and his father. How his father might've tried to be a better person but wouldn't or couldn't. How Edwin lived his life sheltering his mother from the town's gossip. I wondered what his life had been like. It seemed fairly empty and lonely. I hoped his life might get better, now, but I didn't really expect it to. Nobody can change a town with just a few words. I wondered why he stayed.

Finally, I realized it wasn't all that important whether or not I understood Skunk, or Mr. King for that matter, as long as I understood that there was more to them (and everybody else, I guess) than most people wanted to believe.

VII. Gethsemane

I should've known something was up; I watched *Miami Vice*. I mean, the signs were all there. Me and Emily had been seeing each other for about three months on Sunday nights because I had school during the week and she worked late most every weekend night. I knew it'd be a long row to hoe seeing Emily regular. She'd never had much as far as a happy childhood, what with her mama being dead and her daddy being such a jerk. Not to mention the shit Gardener'd gotten her into when she first ran away from home. I knew it wouldn't be easy, but after I laid down the law with Gardener and kicked his drug-dealing ass off my place, I figured things would straighten up for Emily. I knew I loved her, and I'd burn in Hell before I'd let anything else bad happen to her.

I even tried to get her to quit working at the diner, but she kept on about having to do something to put food on her table. I had to admit she had a point. My dad still didn't know she was out there on our property, and she'd been there so long now I couldn't rightly bring it up. Even if I did, he wasn't about to let the girl I was seeing move in with us. He'd probably put her in foster care or something, and Emily'd die before she'd agree to that. So keep working she did, and we saw each other on Sunday nights.

I should've known something was wrong, but as usual, I had my head stuck up my ass.

My largest weakness, I think, is a frustrating habit of sticking my head there when I least need to. It never fails that by the time I pull it out again all hell's broken loose, and there's precious little I can do to fix it.

School was almost over. Really over. I had managed to successfully complete my public education. (Admittedly English, math, and science had been hairy, but art, P. E., and agriculture had been a breeze.) Now, I had thought that graduation would spell the end of all my worries. I'd been educated; now I just had to find me a house, a job, and a wife, in no particular order, and it'd be smooth sailing from here on out.

My Dad, though, had other ideas.

"You can't do jack shit without a degree, son. I reckon you better rethink your plans and work college in there somewhere."

When was this going to end? He'd said almost the same thing when I wanted to drop out of school three years ago. All the "jack shit" crap, the diploma stuff, and again with the rethinking business. How far was he going to take this?

"Besides," he added, "if you want a girl, you better get you a smart one, or else you're both in trouble. The smart ones go to college."

Well, May rolled around and everybody'd been accepted somewhere. Parry was going to Vanderbilt to study law. Christy Davis got accepted to Columbia. Hell, rumor had it that Gardener Smith had been hired by the Catagua County Sheriff's Department when he graduated from the police academy in Fulton County the previous month. (Of course, if Gardener had gotten a sudden respect for the law of the land, I didn't reckon there was much point in anybody else going anywhere. We were obviously in The Last Days and Christ, Himself, was on His way.) Everybody had gotten into somewhere, that is, except me.

The thing was, though, I'd done convinced myself I wanted to go to college. Dad had spent so much time talking about fraternities, parties, and pretty, smart girls, I felt I'd be putting myself out if I didn't go on and further myself. It'd just figure that as soon as I wanted a higher education, I couldn't have it. This always happened. If I wanted something, I either never could get it, or I'd lose interest once I had it.

Finally, two weeks before graduation, I received a letter of acceptance from Bedford Forrest State College in Bartow, Georgia. Admittedly, it was the last college I'd applied to, but it was also the first to accept me, and I didn't expect any others to put up fierce competition for me. My dad was thrilled with the letter and brochure, especially the parts about "a fine institution that honors the Southern heritage while providing an Ivy League education at an affordable price."

The only person not terribly thrilled with the prospect of my going away was Emily.

"What the hell you want to go all the way out there to Bartow for?" She inhaled deeply on her cigarette and looked out into the woods. "Ain't you had enough schoolin'?"

I thought about the fraternities, parties, and pretty, smart girls. "I don't think a fella can have too much schooling," I replied, trying to sound like I believed it. "Way things are going, nowadays, pretty much everybody's gonna need more schooling. Hell, I bet you can't even sell crack without some kinda business degree."

"I wouldn't know about that," she said under her breath. "Cain't you go somewhere closer? I mean Bartow's like three hours away. Why don't you go to Catagua Tech and be a plumber or something? It ain't but twenty, thirty miles away. You could stay here and get your education if you're so all fired anxious to get one."

I wasn't too sure, but I strongly suspected that Catagua Tech didn't have much to offer by way of parties and fraternities, and even if they had any smart, pretty plumbers, I probably didn't want one.

"I don't know, Emily, I just don't want to spend my entire existence right here. I want to experience something before I die. I want to have some kind of life."

"Listen, buddy boy," I could tell, she was getting irritable now because she hardly ever called me that, "take it from somebody who knows. Experience ain't all it's cracked up to be. I've told you before, it's a big bad world out there and you ain't half ready for it. You don't know shit about shit."

"Yeah, well, Missy, maybe you're right." I was getting pissed, myself, now. "But just remember this one thing, if it wasn't for me, you'd be dead now or still selling yourself for Gardener."

"Yeah, I been meaning to thank you for that." She sounded anything but thankful, though. "It was *such* a help. You should be pleased with yourself."

"I didn't have to do it, you know."

"You didn't go unrewarded."

"I didn't ask to be, Emily."

"No. No you didn't. You didn't say no either."

"Maybe I should have. I thought you wanted to do it."

"See? You're blind. Shit about shit, boy. Shit about shit."

I stood up and leaned into her face. "I may not know shit about shit, but at least I ain't afraid to find out."

She pushed me away, stood up, and turned towards the door. "Go on, go off to college, get your 'higher education.' But you remember this: Smart people'll cut you just as deep as morons. Nice people hurt you worse than assholes."

"Maybe I better leave," I said quietly. I didn't feel so good.

"I think you should." She opened the door.

I turned to go. "I'll see you next week."

The door closed behind me.

I got to skip school the next Wednesday and Thursday because the college was offering a free tour and orientation. It would take two days, and I'd get to stay in a real dorm room and experience the "college life" first hand.

I didn't tell Emily I was going. There wasn't time, really. I'd already seen her the previous Sunday. I guess I could've left a message for her at Hell's Ditch, but Big Bob Crumb bitched something awful whenever he had to do anything remotely nice. "I ain't no goddamned message service." I could hear him say.

Besides, she'd made her feelings about me and my education terribly clear.

Bedford Forrest was a dream come true. I got there early and wandered all over the campus. Dad wasn't kidding about the girls. I'd never seen so many all together in one place before. They sat and talked about all kinds of stuff on the stairs of all the buildings. They lounged around on the hills in the quad area smoking cigarettes and drinking coffee.

"Cappuccino," a particularly attractive redhead informed me when I asked where she had gotten her coffee. "Over at the student center."

I must have looked lost because she offered to take me there herself. When we got there, I invited her to sit with me, but she said she had "some terribly important ... stuff" to take care of before her class at five o'clock.

About ten o'clock, I went to the admissions office to check in. There was a bunch of forms and stuff to fill out, a couple of lines to stand in, more forms to fill out ("correctly this time, please"), and finally, they stuck one of them "Hello my name is" stickers with the wrong name on it to my shirt. It didn't seem worth it to complain. I looked out for someone with my name tag, but I must have been absent or something, so I remained "Jerald Oakley" all day.

They took me and a group of about fifteen all around the campus that day. Everywhere we went I saw beautiful girls. Outside on the lawn, sitting in the classrooms, even one standing on the roof of the library with a camera.

I saw the redhead again as we stopped in front of the Social Sciences building. She was walking with this big guy who looked like some kind of terrorist. He had short clipped hair, and he swaggered. She looked like she was getting on to him about something or other, but he didn't take no notice, just kept looking for a building to bomb or a bus to hijack. Finally, she walked off from him all huffed up. Our guide finished whatever it was he was saying, and we went on to lunch where a fairly attractive blonde sat two tables over.

When the tour was over, we went to our dorm rooms and got settled in. We'd all been invited to a party out in Nathan Valley that night to celebrate the end of Spring Quarter, so I was anxious to unpack my stuff and get on out there. I had brought my favorite denim shirt, my special belt with the guitar-shaped buckle, and my lucky jacket for just such an occasion, and after a quick shower, shave, and Binaca blast, I was ready to go.

Now, I'd been to some parties in my time, but these were mainly just some friends and acquaintances gathered at somebody's house whose parents were out of town. About all we'd do was play music too loud, drink cheap beer and Boone's Farm wine until we puked, and run out into the woods when somebody called the cops. Nothing prepared me for the pagan festival I found in Nathan Valley.

There must've been a good two hundred folks out there of all ages and description wandering around. Some were grouped in their own little sub-parties and passing joints back and forth. I could see others heading for the tree line in pairs and groups of three or four. There was a stage erected at the far end of the valley between two towers of speakers, and four guys were dancing around on it playing Pink Floyd, The Grateful Dead, and Whitesnake. Near the stage several folks were dancing and swaying to the music. Somebody thrust a plastic cup in my hand as I headed towards the band.

When I reached the edge of the dance area, I noticed the red-headed girl on the other side. She seemed terribly irritated about something, and sure enough, the Terrorist showed up beside her and put his arm on her shoulder. She shrugged him off and ignored him as he shrank back into the crowd. I kept watching her until she caught my eye and came over.

"Hey," I said when she was near enough to hear. "Fancy meeting you here."

"Do what?" She seemed distracted and glanced back over to the Terrorist. He stared at her intently.

"I said, 'Fancy meeting you here.'"

"Yeah, whatever." She glanced back at the Terrorist then took my hand, set my cup on the stage, and drug me towards the dancers. "Look, you wanna dance or what?"

Now, I'm not the greatest dancer in the world, but I didn't feel too uncomfortable dancing with all these people around. I was, quite frankly, impressed with my ability to snag a date so quickly. Dad was right. This was my element. I'd only been here a day and already pretty, smart girls were throwing themselves at me. I was taking them away from their boyfriends even. Like candy from a baby.

"What's your name, darlin'?" I asked trying to be all cool and stuff.

"Huh?" She was looking over my shoulder, obviously gloating to everybody who missed out on me. "Oh, Julie."

I told her my name and that it was a pleasure to meet her.

"Whatever. Move closer to the edge." She began leading me to the far end of the dancing area. I could see the Terrorist lurking a few feet away and glowering at us, but I didn't care. Julie had made her choice; let him suffer.

After a while, Julie began to grind into me in time with the music. I can't say I minded. I even got a little excited when I realized the Terrorist was still watching the whole thing. Finally, just before the band finished its set, Julie pulled my head to hers and kissed me. I looked back at the terrorist with a silly grin on my face, but he was storming off through the crowd. I turned back to Julie, but she was moving away, too.

"Hey," I said, "where are you going?"

"Look kid, it's been real. Maybe I'll see you around."

"That's cool," I returned. "Maybe I'll catch you tomorrow morning or..." But she had already left. I made my way back to my plastic cup and spent the rest of the party reveling in my conquest.

The next morning, as I was on my way to breakfast, I saw Julie walking towards me. I waved, but she turned and entered a car before I could reach her. Later that day, I saw her and the Terrorist outside the library all up in each other's laps kissing and fondling each other. I could take a hint.

As I walked past the building, trying hard not to look at the couple, the Terrorist looked up.

"Hey, buddy." I tried to ignore him. "Hey, boy, I'm talking to you."

I looked back in their direction. The Terrorist had a smug grin on his face, and Julie looked for all the world like her mouth had been surgically attached to his neck.

"You enjoy your dance last night, kid?"

No answer.

"Thought you were the big rooster in the hen house last night, didn't you?" The Terrorist's grin got bigger. "Yeah, baby," he said to Julie, "right there." He turned his attention back to me. "You sure are quiet, boy. What's wrong? Did you really think you and my girl were some kind of item? Like she could possibly be interested in a pimply-faced little teenager who ain't even out of high school yet."

I couldn't say anything. I wanted to, but I couldn't come up with a comeback, and my mouth wouldn't work right, either. I just stood there with my mouth opening and closing. Finally, I just turned around and began to walk off.

Julie's voice was the last straw. "Hey, *darlin*,'" she said drawling out the last word like some backwoods hick. I stopped but didn't turn around. "A little advice for you. Denim shirts and giant belt buckles went out with disco." Then she started giggling and kept on until I was out of earshot.

The next day was graduation day. It should have been the best day of my life; I should have been excited. But I couldn't quit thinking about the humiliation of the day before. All day long I just kept replaying it over and over again. I couldn't concentrate on the hangman game Mr. King conducted during English. I lost track of the movie we watched during math class. I kept falling out of step during graduation practice, and Miss Grumbald would yell at me. I couldn't hardly do anything because of what happened.

I'd never experienced anything like that. Christy Davis had yelled at me and made me feel guilty and stuff when she broke up with me for cheating on her, but she'd never made me feel small. I don't think Emily, as irritable as she could be, would have ever insulted me that bad. After all, her irritability and shortness was due more to the threat of me leaving than anything. She might snap at me and make snide comments, but she'd never make fun of me. She'd never laugh at me.

And that decided me. I left school that afternoon, and had no plans to come back that night. To hell with them. To hell with Dad, with college, and with smart, pretty girls. There's more important things in life than all that crap. Emily may not be all that book smart, but she's pretty, and she's got a hell of a lot more common sense than most girls twice her age. More importantly, she wants me to stay with her. So that's where I'll go. To hell with school and graduation. Miss Grimbald's just gonna hiss and point at me when I get out of step anyway.

I knew Emily couldn't ordinarily see me on any other day but Sunday, so I didn't really expect to find her at home. Since it was a Friday night, I figured she'd be at work, and I'd just sit around the shack and wait for her. As I neared the place, though, I began to get a weird floating feeling in my stomach.

As I drew closer to the shack, I saw a light on in the bedroom window. There wasn't a sound in the little clearing, what Skunk Wilson would've called "graveyard quiet." If Emily was at work, someone might be going through her stuff. I picked up a tree branch from the ground and inched as silently as possible to the window.

At first I couldn't see anything through the window, but I could hear someone whimpering and mumbling something I couldn't quite make out. I rubbed my sleeve across the glass to clear away some of the grime and get a better looksee at who was in there.

The sinking feeling in my stomach began rising as my mind became a sheet of white. Without thinking I swung the branch at the window shattering the glass and splintering the frame. I pushed what was left of the window up, scrambled through (cutting myself something awful on the glass), and before I knew what had happened, I was running my hands feverishly over Emily's face.

She was naked on her mattress in a pool of blood with her back against the wall. I looked all over her, but I couldn't find where she'd been shot or stabbed or whatever. Her eyes were open, and she was saying something, but she wouldn't answer my questions. She just stared blankly over my shoulder and mumbled. It looked like she'd tried to tie a tourniquet around her arm, but the blood wasn't coming from there. I began examining her legs for a stab wound.

"Oh holy Christ," I mumbled as I opened her legs. The blood was smeared all over her inner thighs. I grabbed a pillow from the mattress and began to press as hard as I could on her groin, but it didn't seem to help. I could feel it soaking through the cotton stuffing.

"Don't tell," she whispered.

"What?"

"Don't tell him, Gardener. I'll fix it." Her words were slow and slurred.

"What are you saying, Emily?"

"Please don't tell Daddy."

The tourniquet was a thick rubber band. Next to the mattress there was a can of sterno, a burned spoon, and a needle.

"Please help me," she whispered.

Her arm was riddled with red punctures.

"Make it stop. I'll fix it, I promise."

A twisted and red coat hanger lay on the other side of the mattress on top of her clothes. Blood was everywhere now.

"Don't tell him, Gardener, him or Daddy." She kept staring blankly over my shoulder.

She'd lied to me. She'd lied to me all along. She couldn't ever change. She'd always be just what she was, a sixteen-year-old prostitute junky, and nothing I could ever do for her would change that. There'd always be somebody bigger than both of us to put her down and start all over again. Oh, I talked big, but I was a coward and everybody knew it: Gardener knew it, Emily knew it, even Julie and the Terrorist knew it.

And now I knew it, too.

For the first time, Emily saw me. "Make it stop," she whispered. Her whole body jerked then, and her mouth foamed as she stared at me with tears in her eyes. "It hurts."

The blood had slowed, but it hadn't stopped. I'd never get her to my car.

She lied to me.

Even if I could, and by some miracle I got her to Catagua General, what would I tell them? I sure couldn't tell them the truth.

She lied to me.

"Do it," she whispered.

I gently pulled her down and lay her across the mattress. Taking the pillow and turning the bloody side towards me, I carefully placed it over her face and applied pressure.

She lied to me.

I couldn't go through with it, though. When she started to twitch and shake, I removed the pillow and wiped the spit off her chin.

"It hurts," she said in a whisper.

"I know," I said and ran my hand over her head trying vainly to smooth her hair.

"Make it stop," she said.

"I can't."

"I'm cold."

I curled up next to her on the mattress and pulled her to me.

In fifteen minutes it was all over. I felt her tremble once more and then nothing. I sat up and rolled her onto her back. She stared past me straight into forever and never said another word.

"I gotta hand it to you, boy. I never in a million years

thought you'd've had the balls to do that."

The voice behind my back scared the hell out of me.

"Looks like you've gone and stepped into a world of trouble, though." Gardener walked from behind me and looked down at Emily. He was wearing a Catagua Deputy's uniform. "Oh well, one good turn deserves another, I reckon. Don't worry, son, I'll take care of everything."

I stood back from the body and stared mutely at Gardener as he went out the back door and returned a minute later with a large canvas tent sack and a plastic ground cloth.

"Wrap it up in that plastic and help me put it in the sack."

I couldn't move and continued to stare at him silently.

"Look here, son. If you ain't gonna help of your own accord, I'll have to motivate you, and I like you too much to do that."

I took the ground cloth and began to unfold it as he picked up the needle and hanger and stuff and put it all in the canvas sack. I didn't say a word as he helped me lift her and fold the plastic over her body. When we stuffed her into the sack, I ignored his remarks about wasting perfectly good camping gear. The zipper caught on some of the plastic, and it took us a while to sort that out.

We drug her out the back door where Gardener had parked his truck and placed her beside the canoe in the bed.

"Grab them cans," Gardener instructed, "and come on back inside."

We doused the bedroom and the living room with gasoline. Before striking the match, though, Gardener stripped to his shorts and doused his uniform, too.

"There's a waste of two weeks' pay."

We went out the back door again, and Gardener had to light three matches before he could get one to stay lit long enough to light the gas.

"Better throw your clothes into the house, too," he said as he opened the driver's door and pulled a tee shirt and a pair of canvas shorts out from behind his seat. "Wear these," he advised. "That much blood ain't gonna do nothing but draw questions." I did as he suggested and went to the passenger side of his truck, but he stopped me. "No, sir," he said, "you need to ride back here and make sure it don't slide out."

I don't remember the drive to the lake. I don't really remember unloading the canoe or Emily. I vaguely recall Gardener tying cement blocks to the bag so "it don't come back."

We put her in the middle of the canoe, pushed it into the water, and climbed into it. We took up oars on either end and paddled to the middle of the lake. Then we lifted her body, trying hard not to overturn the boat, and dropped her into the water before paddling back to the shore.

By the time we drove out of the woods, the entire sky behind us was red and sirens were wailing in the distance.

I didn't say anything as he pulled to a stop at my car.

"Well, I gotta say, boy, you surprised me back there. You stayed calm and didn't wig out under pressure. With a little work, I might be able to get you hired on with me. We could make quite a team."

"No thank you, Gardener," I said as I unlocked my car. "You've helped me out enough for a lifetime."

Epilogue

After I finished my story, they gave me this legal pad and a pen and told me to "write it all down just like you told us." I looked at the legal pad and flipped through its pages before looking questioningly back up.

"Don't worry, sir," they replied, "we have plenty more paper where that came from."

So I began to write, after an hour or two, they came back and told me to take a break and follow them. I put my fingers in their ink and pressed the tips on their paper cards. Then they gave me a bright orange jumpsuit to wear and escorted me to the dining room.

After eating some Salisbury steak with whipped potatoes and cherry pie, I was taken back to the interview room.

Someone had left their newspaper there. Headline: "Sheriff Gardener Smith Brought in by the GBI for Questioning." Before I could get started good, an agent came in.

"You about finished?" he asked. "Your lawyer's here."

"Lawyer?"

Parry stepped in and motioned the agent to leave us alone.

"I got here as soon as I could. Gardener called late yesterday afternoon, but I couldn't get a flight from Nashville until this morning."

"Gardener called?"

"Don't worry, boy," the machine said, *"I'll take care of everything."*

If you walk through the woods, keeping the creek on your left and keep on straight 'til you see the lightning tree what's half dead and bear right, following the foot trail a piece, you'll find a clearing overgrown with weeds and scrub. At the far end of this clearing lies a pile of crumbling brick and a few sheets of rusting tin. This is my place. Obviously, I don't live here or nothing, but it's mine just the same. It's where I go when I want to think about things or just be alone for a while.

I think of rain pattering on a tin roof. Naked, we recline beside each other on the mattress leaning against the wall in the back room lit only by a single hurricane lamp. As her hand runs across my shoulders, I feel her stitches where she sliced the wrong way.

I think of wind whipping around the corners of the shack and chilling us through our clothes, as she sits on the porch and rocks. I sit at her feet, and she runs her hands through my hair. I feel, on my scalp, the stitches where she sliced the wrong way.

I think of fire as I walk away from a burning house. Her hands don't want to go in the bag. I see the stitches where she sliced the wrong way. Someone tugs on my shirt, and I turn to go.

I think of the hard packed earth as I walk from the burning house. Sweat gathering on my brow, a warm wind at my back. Thinking of the stitches where she sliced the wrong way.

Parry tells me I have a good chance to get off. The crime is over fifteen years old; I have ties to the community. He seems to think I may have had extenuating circumstances.

"You have more than a good chance," he told me. "Hell, the judge released you without bail. That's definitely a good sign. You'll get off."

But I'm not sure I want to. I won't be beholden to anybody. I look at my glass of tea sitting on the end table. So easy for it to fall.

And I know which way to slice.

Poems & Other Stories

Fit

I.

When I was six years old, pudgy and awkward,
My grandfather took me fishing for the first time.
He showed me how to hook the worm,
Cast, throw, reel-stop-reel,
Pull in, cast again.
When I caught the fish, it scared me.
Flopping there on the ground
Staring into forever like it knew it was going to die.

II.

My father's father-in-law, large and loud,
Was a good old fashioned country preacher.
Fire and brimstone, hell and damnation, the whole bit.
One Sunday, just before noon, he received the spirit.
Twisting and writhing, and speaking in tongues,
He collapsed before the altar.
While the congregation gave thanks,
He stared beyond us all.

III.

Once, as a teacher, numb and mute,
I watched my student have a seizure.
On the edge of thirty, I stood there like a child
In mute wonder and a little fear
As this sixteen-year-old girl, a mere slip
Jerked and spasmed, twisted and turned.
As her eyes stared straight into forever,
I wondered what they saw.

Icarus Fell

This story is true, except when it isn't:

I

One of my earliest memories is of hearing a story. I don't recall if it was a story told to me in school or at home. On one hand, the overly moralistic message of the tale[1] tends to suggest that it was a dissatisfied schoolmarm trying to control her pupils with irrational fear. However, equally suggestive is my father and grandfather's appreciation of Greek myths. The source of the tale, though, is irrelevant. It's the tale itself that bears import.

Daedalus and his son Icarus had offended King Minos[2] and were imprisoned in an insoluble labyrinth (compasses not having been invented yet)[3]. They had wandered about for years ... months ... days ... hours ... well, for an awfully long time when Daedalus remembered that he had two pairs of wings in his knapsack and some wax with which to attach them. Now, since no one had told them that man cannot fly with only some feathers on a stick and a dab of wax, Daedalus and Icarus put the wings on and easily flew out the top of the maze to safety.

Well, one of them did anyway. Daedalus showed Icarus how to operate the wings and told him all about the Gulf Stream, electrical storms, and seagulls and how to avoid these various dangers. He also told him of the worst danger: the sun. You see wax isn't really the best adhesive to use in aerodynamics, having, as it does, such a low melting

---

[1] Dealing with the idea that when youth disregards the dictates and suggestions of age, chaos, death, and spankings ensue.

[2] Perhaps they made him invisible clothes, stole his firstborn, or ate his porridge. The how and why's are unimportant.

[3] I remember that upon asking how they got in the inescapable maze to begin with, I was told "magic" which I took to mean, "I don't know, shut-up, and listen to the story."

temperature[4]. He told Icarus several times slowly and clearly not to fly too near the sun because the wax would melt and he'd plummet to the sea quicker than the stock market on Black Tuesday.

"Don't worry, Dad," Icarus replied with the usual nerve-wracking apathy common to adolescents, "you tell me this stuff all the time. 'Don't fly near the sun, or you'll fall to the sea. Wait thirty minutes until you fly, or you'll fall to the sea. Clean your room, or you'll fall to the sea.' I get it." And Icarus took off.

Well, you know what happened. Icarus flew up and up. He turned loopedy-loops and barrel rolls, dives and twists.

"Man, this is cool," he thought as he soared through the heavens experiencing a thrill that only a select few[5] have known. He felt like a god. As he flew, he marveled at the beauty that was the earth. He saw farmers plowing their fields, fishermen pulling in their nets, and irate townspeople burning the IRS man at the stake. He beheld the whole of the planet at once. He saw "the big picture" in all its entirety, and it was amazing. Enthralling.

Of course, he forgot all about the wings and the wax and the sun. He flew higher and higher in order to see more and more of this enrapturing vision. He'd never felt so free, so happy. Higher he flew and higher.

The sun melted his wings, and Icarus plummeted to the sea. The ocean swallowed him, and he died with a beatific smile upon his face.

Daedalus, grief-stricken and, it must be said, a little pissed at his hard-headed son, flew on to Sicily where he lived out the end of his days secure on terra firma and as far away from the sea as he could get on a small Italian island.

---

[4] If you don't believe me, I dare you to find any Johnson's wax on the space shuttle.

[5] Those with no innate sense of danger.

When I was in second grade, my parents divorced. Dad got his car, his clothes, and two child-support bills. Mom got my brother, John, and me. She then moved us from Moreland to Union City. We lived in a condominium in a gated community named Shannon Villas[6]. I hated it until I met my next door neighbor, a seven-year-old boy named Jeffrey, who lived with his mother and older brother, Derek[7]. He was a shy boy who never said much. I saw him jumping up and down on the sidewalk one Saturday morning, and when I asked what he was doing, he told me he thought he could fly.

Well, he knew he couldn't fly yet, but he believed that he could, one day, fly if he met a series of requirements.

"You have to be really good," he told me once as we walked home from school, "and you have to truly believe you can."

"Jeffrey," I replied, "you're the best kid around. You do your homework. You're polite to the grown-ups. You don't ever talk back, or get into fights, or anything[8]."

"Well, apparently, I'm not good enough because I know I believe."

So he practiced and he practiced. He'd jump off the first step in a stairwell and flap his arms as hard as he could. When

---

[6] Gated communities tickle me. We put a guardhouse with a rising gate at every entrance and put up wall to rival Berlin's around the neighborhood (making the entire structure appear like some concentration camp for the upper middle class) so that no one who doesn't belong can get in. The premise is that this will keep the "bad element" out of our neighborhoods and protect us from thieves, muggers, and vandals. In my experience, though, this practice simply makes it easier for the thieves, muggers, and vandals who already live there to terrorize the neighborhood with no fear of reprisal.

[7] Jeffrey and Derek's father had died a few years previous after being hit by a car as he crossed the road. They never caught the driver.

[8] Once Cecil Barker, the school bully, caught Jeffrey jumping off stairwells and flapping his arms. For some reason, Cecil took this as a personal affront and proceeded to beat the tar out of Jeffrey for "being a freak." Jeffrey just took it; he didn't fight back. He didn't even cry, he just stood there with a calm smile on his face, and Cecil soon grew tired and walked away. Jeffrey returned to jumping off the stairs as if nothing had happened.

he felt he had stayed in the air longer than he normally would have, he'd move up to the next step. Three times a week we would lay flat on his older brother's weight bench and do butterflies and laterals to build up the strength in his arms.

"You have to be physically able to fly, too. All the goodness and belief in the world won't help if you don't have the strength to hold yourself up."

He was a good swimmer; his father had taught him a few years before the accident. He felt like swimming was the closest thing most people had to flying. He was like a seal. He'd slip into the water so smoothly there'd be hardly a ripple. He could stay under longer than anybody I'd ever seen. He must have had the lungs of a whale. He preferred swimming in the ocean to swimming in a pool, though, because "the currents in the sea are a lot like the air streams in the sky. If I learned to move in those," he explained, "the Gulf Stream'll be no problem."

I remember one night we snuck out of our houses, and he took me to this place in the woods, The Devil's Playground, he called it. It was supposed to be a circle of trees within which nothing would grow. Sometimes, if you believed hard enough[9] and if the moon was right, you could, so long as you were very, very quiet, sneak up and see the Devil dancing in the trees[10]. We were just about there when I tripped on an exposed tree root and knocked Jeffrey down the hill. When he hit the bottom he couldn't move his leg. I had to go get his mother, who in turn, called my mother. Both of them and Derek had to come out and help carry Jeffrey back. He'd broken one leg, sprained the other ankle, and fractured an arm.

"This is just great," he said as Derek fashioned a splint. At first, I thought that he was being sarcastic, but he continued.

---

[9] Yeah, Jeffrey was real big on the whole power of belief thing. I've often thought that he would've made a great preacher because his belief was contagious. Of course, things being like they are he'd be labeled a dangerous cult, and the Feds would burn down his "compound" in order to protect the common herd.

[10] We never saw him ourselves, but Jeffrey always blamed it on my "heavy soled, clod-hopping hiking boots."

"Broken bones heal back stronger than they were before. I'll be able to fly in no time."

"Oh my god," his mother said, "he's delirious, I bet he has a concussion."

He never did grow out of his belief. He never really flew either. A couple of years later, Jeffrey fell from the roof of the school, broke his collarbone, shattered his spine, and died. They said he'd lost his balance and slipped over the side. At his funeral, his mother commented that he looked "like an angel on a cloud."

The last time we spoke was when we were both in fifth grade, shortly after my mother remarried and moved us all to Fort Polk, Louisiana, to live with our new stepfather. John and I had come back to spend Thanksgiving with our grandparents.

We were sitting on the roof of the elementary school[11]. Fall was drawing to a close, and the leaves had turned from orange and yellow to brown. Very few were left in the trees, actually. They made, instead, a soft carpet all over the schoolyard.

"You still trying to fly?" I asked him as we watched the cars pass slowly down the street.

"Yeah, sometimes. Not as much, though. I don't have as much time anymore." He stood up and looked down at the schoolyard spread below him and smiled. "It would still be cool though. I haven't given up. Maybe one day."

III

When I was in my mid-twenties and working on my master's thesis in English, I read an awful lot of existential philosophy. Now, this was not the first time I had been exposed to existentialism; it was just the first time I came even close to understanding any of it. One writer in particular, Albert Camus,

---

[11] We had discovered years ago that if you were very careful, you could climb up the rear drainpipe and shuffle over the awning onto the roof. This was where we hid out on Saturday afternoons to avoid doing our chores.

a Frenchman, began to fascinate me. It was through his most famous essay that I learned the story of Sisyphus[12].

Having upset the gods[13], Sisyphus was condemned by Zeus to push a heavy stone up a mountain.

"When you get the rock to the top," Zeus informed him, "you can stop and rest, not before."

He toiled and toiled pushing the stone but an inch every day. He didn't get coffee breaks. He didn't get time-and-a-half. He just got sore. Up he'd push this big heavy stone.

Day after day, year after year, Sisyphus worked and pushed and toiled and sweated. In life, Sisyphus had been a weak man both physically and spiritually. Now though, his muscles rippled in the glow cast by Hades' eternal fire. He grew in stature as he stretched himself beyond the limits of physical exertion. He became impressed with the extension of his own endurance. His confidence in his own abilities grew.

Now, I'm not saying everything was peachy for Sisyphus. Obviously, he couldn't ever sleep for fear that he'd lose the boulder, so he had a tendency towards irritability. More importantly, though, for the same reason that he couldn't sleep, Sisyphus couldn't bathe either. As a result, he had acquired somewhat of a smell.

It took him ten years to roll the boulder up the mountain. With one final shove, the rock moved over the final rise and Sisyphus was done. Unfortunately, as he looked around for something with which to block the stone, a little black bird alit on the rock. The weight was too much, and the rock rolled all the way back down the hill.

Sisyphus, feeling discouraged ran as fast as he could down the hill, hoping to overtake the boulder before it reached the bottom. He tripped, though, lost his balance, and tumbled all

---

[12] The essay is titled, originally enough, *The Myth of Sisyphus*.

[13] Again, the how and why's are irrelevant. Gods don't really need reasons for their actions; they're gods. What's the point in being a god if you have to justify yourself to common human beings?

the way down, too. He landed next to the boulder at the foot of the mountain. He then stood up, dusted himself off, and began pushing the stone back to the top.

Ten years later, it happened again. And ten years after that. And ten years after that. After the fifth time it happened, Sisyphus came to realize that he would never get the stone to rest forever at the top of the mountain. Something would always knock it back down, and he'd have to push it up again. He shrugged his shoulders, dusted himself off, and with a spring in his step and a smile on his face, Sisyphus began the never-ending job of pushing his rock up the mountain.

Requiem

I don't remember the first time I met her. Maybe it was art class, maybe drama. I was in eleventh grade, though. I do remember that.

(It was art class, Darwin. First period, first semester. You sat way on the other side of the table drinking Coca-Cola and laughing with Byron Bent.)

I also remember that she was the most beautiful girl I had ever seen.

(What about Chastity? I thought she was the most beautiful girl you ever met.)

No, no. Chastity couldn't hold a candle to Elena Luna. Chastity was good looking and everything, some would go as far as hot...

(I wouldn't. I thought she looked like a slut, really. Too much make-up and the whole fluttering eyelash thing whenever a guy so much as glanced at her. Honestly, Darwin, I never knew what you saw in her.)

You didn't know her like I did.

(And you didn't know her like every other male on campus did.)

Shut-up. I'm not interested in Chastity right now.

(That's a first.)

May I continue please?

(By all means.)

It was, indeed, art class. I sat next to Byron, right across the room from Elena. If memory serves, Byron was giving me unsolicited advice on my love life. He always blamed my insistence on wearing black berets and denim jackets for my lack of popularity with the fairer sex. Byron, who worshipped the ground Prince walked on, felt I'd do much better with some "uptown threads" favoring the color purple.

(Hah.)

I remember looking up at one point to see the olive complexioned girl across the room smiling at me. Her long brown hair hung over one eye as she slowly lowered her head and continued to smile at me over her glasses. She wore a full-length white dress made of some flimsy material under a denim vest, and she had braided dried flowers into her hair. She looked for all the world like a little wood nymph. I smiled back; then she turned and said something to the girl sitting next to her and giggled. I can't for the life of me remember the other girl's name.

(Jesus, Darwin, it was Amy, Amy O'Brien. She was only your first real girlfriend. What's the matter with you?)

I can't really remember a time when Elena wasn't laughing or smiling.

(I can. Several, in fact. You never heard the screaming and yelling that went on in that house. The drunken father yells at his wife. The wife yells back. The inevitable crack of flesh hitting flesh. The brother yelling at the father. Another slap. The daughters hide out in the bedrooms playing music to drown out the screams.)

After that first day, I was smitten.

(You talked about the new girl all night long and drove your folks crazy. It was always "Elena this" "Elena that." You waxed poetic for a full hour about her smile alone. Your dad was convinced that you'd kill yourself if this Elena person so much as stared at you cross-eyed.)

Which she did quite a bit, I remember.

(It was fun, shut up. So you were "smitten"; why didn't you do anything about it?)

I asked her out a few of times. I took her to a couple of movies. I bought her dinner. Hell, I drove ten miles out of my way every morning to give her a lift to school.

(You never so much as held hands.)

She could have reached for mine just as easily as I could hers.

(Darwin Mayflower, now that's just a copout, and you know it. I was a good Catholic girl; I could never be that forward. Admit it; you were scared.)

I was not! I just didn't think you were interested in me that way. You never gave me any indication.

(I gave you my rosary.)

Big fucking deal. You gave me a crucifix with some beads on it. So what?

(You don't remember why, do you? Well, let me refresh your memory. You and Keif and Cassady Nelson crashed some party, and you all decided to steal something from the house before you left. Keif stole a hairbrush, Cassady took a bottle of bleach, and you snuck into one of the bedrooms and grabbed a rosary off the dresser. Remember?)

Yeah, I remember.

(Do you remember what happened the next Monday when you came to pick me up?)

...

(Do you?)

Why don't you tell it? You're doing it better than I would.

(You bragged about it! Like it was some kind of honor to have stolen someone's religious icon. For a while I thought you were the biggest asshole God had ever given a body to. I began to cry, and you stopped the car.

("Elena, what's wrong?" You kept asking it over and over, but you never tried to hold me.)

I didn't think it was appropriate.

(Like it was appropriate to steal the rosary?)

Well, you were obviously pissed at me; I didn't think I was the one you'd really want comfort from.

(You just didn't think. You never did. I'm not sure you've learned that lesson yet. Miescha, Monique, Jennifer. They've all told you the same thing, but you never listen.)

We were talking about the rosary.

(I told you to give it back. We skipped school that day and you drove out to the house and put the rosary in their mailbox.

I told you that you couldn't just go around stealing people's faith because it was fun. I said you could only have someone's rosary if it was given to you in love. Then I reached into my pocket and gave you mine. So don't sit there and tell me I never gave you any indication that I cared for you. I gave you my fucking rosary because I loved you and didn't want you to burn in Hell for something so stupid as a childish prank.)

If you were so in love with me, then why'd you tell me you loved Keif?

(I thought I did.)

Well, there you go then. How could you love me *and* Keif?

(Did you love Chastity?)

No.

(Darwin.)

Alright. Yes I did, but what does that have to do with the price of eggs?

(Did you love me?)

With almost every fiber of my being.

(Well, there you go, then. I loved both of you. And I tried to explain this, but as usual you wouldn't listen. All you heard was "I'm in love with Keif Nelson," and you tuned me out. You took me home, and you never, ever asked me out again. Oh, we hung out still. We even held hands sometimes, but I always instigated it. You didn't try to understand; you just turned your back on me and retreated into your shell.)

What else could I have done, Elena? You seem to know so Goddamned much! You liked Keif; he liked you. Keif was one of my best friends. What chance did I have?

(More than you could ever know.)

I knew Keif was seeing someone else, but he didn't like her. I couldn't come between my best friend and you. Tell me, Miss Luna. Just what exactly were my options?

(You could have kept trying. You could have listened to me. I was fifteen years old, Darwin. You could have hung in there and shown me that you cared.)

That's asking a lot of me.

(No more than you're capable of, no matter what opinion you hold of yourself.)

On the day they buried you, I felt my whole world disintegrate. I watched your casket lowered into the ground, and I couldn't stop screaming. I was like some old Jew at the Wailing Wall. I was a wild animal. I fell to the ground writhing and screaming.

(I remember.)

It was as if I suddenly realized my time was up. I had waited too long, and now it was over. I shouted to Heaven at the injustice.

"Don't let her go in!" I screamed. "I haven't said good bye, yet." Over and over, it was all I could get out between gasps for air and the sobbing.

(I heard you.)

Finally, Yonah and Gus had to carry me to the car.

(But you came back later. After you had calmed down and the other mourners had left. You knelt by my grave and cried silently.)

I told you again, how much I loved you, but it was too late.

(No it wasn't. Then you reached into your pocket and pulled out the rosary.)

I said a "Hail Mary."

(Well, a reasonable facsimile thereof.)

I did the best I could under the circumstances. When I finished, I dug a small hole over your grave, scratching the loose dirt with my fingers, and I placed the rosary there before re-filling the hole and driving home.

(You can only have someone's rosary if it's given to you in love.)

Too bad it was too late.

(It wasn't too late, Darwin. I keep telling you that, and you keep not listening.)

Of course it's too late; you're dead, now.

(But you're not.)

Hand-Me-Down Boy

Nothing I own
Is my own.

Submitted for your perusal:

One rickety bedframe
Of my grandparents,
Used to conceive a family then
Passed down to me.

Two mattresses, slightly used,
Given by my roommate's ex-girlfriend.

Three dressers, varnish peeled,
Left by my wife
With me as an afterthought.

A desk built by my nth great-grandfather...
Well, his slaves.

Some bookcases and a dolphin
Built and created by Monica.

My great-grandmother's rocker,
Her daughter's throne,
My sister's futon,
And Jay's T.V.

I own:
       -my brother's wardrobe
       -my cousin's sheets
       -my father's car and
       -my ex-wife's table and chairs
but not my name.

I have:
      -my mother's eyes
      -my uncle's hair
      -my grandfather's
          caustic tongue and
      -my father's
          overwhelming feelings
of inadequacy and guilt.

Oh well,
      It's their loss.

Love Ever Yearns

"You wouldn't believe the day I had," Rayne Grisham announces to his wife as he slumps into the La-Z-Boy recliner and pops open a Coors. His wife, Christy, says nothing.

"First off," he turns the can up and takes a long swig, "none of the little brats had done their work. Again. I don't care how many friggin' times I tell them; it's like talking to the moon. They just sit there like stone and don't say a word."

Christy sits there like stone and doesn't say a word.

"Then, Alex comes in to observe me today of all days. Students haven't read, half the class is out anyway, half of what's there keeps nodding off, but he wants to dock me for making them read in class. What the hell else am I supposed to do?" Rayne does not pause for a reply. "I mean, I wasn't even supposed to *be* there today. You'd think they'd let a guy off for his anniversary. They could've covered my classes. Of all days."

He sits back in silence and turns on the television news. Christy doesn't seem to mind.

It is the same old miserable song: death, plague, dissension, depravity, and squalor. Rayne flips through the channels, watching a little of each newscast. Enough to know he doesn't particularly want to know more. He does pay more attention to the local news when he sees Thomas Calloway, the school janitor, being led off camera by police officers.

"Hey," he turns to his wife, "didn't you use to date him?"

Again, no reply from Christy. Rayne settles into channel surfing for a few more hours. Then, a little after seven, he rises and goes to the kitchen.

"What do you feel like, honey?" He calls from the refrigerator. "We got plenty. I can make us up something nice if you want. I mean it *is* our anniversary and all. How about some pasta and vegetables? I can make some garlic bread to go with it, maybe have some Merlot to top it off?"

Rayne waits for about ten seconds. When no answer seems forthcoming, he pulls out a Tupperware dish covered in aluminum foil and looks inside. Half a meatloaf with ketchup. He absently sets it on the counter and looks in the fridge again. A few slices of loaf bread (the heels and two other slices) with the neck of the bag wrapped around them twice because the wire twist is missing, a mayonnaise jar with barely anything in it, and a jar containing two flaccid pickles floating forlornly in their brine. All this goes on the counter next to the meatloaf.

"Last chance for real food," he calls out to the living room. Not surprisingly, Christy still refuses to answer. "All right," he sighs, "leftovers it is."

He slices the meatloaf in half, spreads what is left of the mayo on the bread, and sandwiches the meat between the slices. Putting the two sandwiches on one plate, Rayne then pulls the last paper towel from the roll and tucks it under the plate in his hand. He tucks the pickle jar under an arm, and with one hand holding the sandwiches, he grabs an open bag of chips with his free hand before returning to the living room. This time he sits on the sofa next to his wife and places the food carefully upon the coffee table. He tunes the television to The Discovery Channel, and as he eats his sandwich, he watches what's left of a documentary on advances in radiation therapy.

Afterwards, he switches over to CBS for the final episode of *Murphy Brown*. It used to be Christy's favorite show, but now she seems uninterested. He leaves it on anyway. Christy also hasn't touched her sandwich.

"Not hungry?" he asks as he takes a bite of hers. "Well, I hate to see food go to waste; you know that."

After *Chicago Hope*, a rerun that had something or other to do with a double mastectomy (he only half watched it), Rayne leaves the news on to see if he can catch any more of the Thomas Calloway story, but quickly grows bored. Just another mundane murder, this time he happens to know the accused. After the news (even the weather report is the same: fair), Rayne stands and carries the dishes and garbage back to the

149

kitchen. The plate goes into the sink, the pickle jar and paper towel into the trashcan.

He yawns when he returns to the living room and stretches his arms over his head.

"Well, I guess I'll go on to bed. You coming?"

When he receives no answer, Rayne picks Christy up and gently carries her upstairs to the bedroom.

He can see her in the mirror as he washes his face and brushes his teeth. He smiles at her, aquamarine toothpaste foaming out of his mouth like a psychedelic, rabid dog.

"Ahh rhuvv rhu," he grins briefly, then spits into the sink. When his words receive no response, his grin slowly fades. *She used to love that.* He flips off the bathroom light. *Used to tickle her to death.*

He walks over to her before crawling into bed and softly rubs his hand across her smooth surface. She gleams in the moonlight streaming through the window.

"Happy anniversary, sweetheart," he whispers as he places her ever so gently on his bedside table. He sets the alarm for six a.m. and closes his eyes. The last things he sees before drifting off are the words etched across her middle:

Christine Patrice Davis-Grisham
Beloved wife and daughter
1971-1998

Negative Space

She had been gone two months when her mother called to invite me to Thanksgiving dinner. The invitation surprised me, though I suppose it shouldn't have. From the time I met them, Jessi's parents tried to make me feel a part of the family. On a cold day in February, eight months after Jessi and I met, we moved in together. I felt weird about going to her parents' house to get her things, but as soon as I walked in, Grace gave me a hug and ushered me into the sitting room for coffee. Jessi's father, Jimmy, met me in the kitchen. He stood over me in his dusty overalls and workboots, glowering from under his wide-brimmed hat with a look that said, "You must be the low-down son of a bitch who's taking my little girl away," and chewing on the remains of a cigar.

I tried to stammer a greeting, something to reassure him that my intentions toward his daughter were honorable (a tricky thing considering we were just about to shack up together). In the South, especially Owen, Georgia, it's imperative for a prospective suitor to impress his intended's father with assertiveness and confidence.

I stammered like Porky Pig and stared at the space between my head and the floor.

Then I noticed a callused hand stretching out into my line of sight, and when I looked up, he was grinning around his cigar. "Welcome to the family, son. Keep her straight, now."

All that aside, I still felt awkward with the idea of spending Thanksgiving with the family of my now estranged wife, so I declined.

"Now, Aleck," Grace sounded like she was scolding a small child for getting his Sunday pants grassy. "There's no need for you to be spending the holidays alone."

"I won't be alone," I lied, "I got some people coming over."

I could tell Grace saw through my scam. I could picture her on the other end, leaning against the doorframe with the phone cradled between her shoulder and cheek as she stared sadly at my picture in the den holding her right arm across her chest so that her hand supported her left elbow while she idly twisted a gray-streaked strand of black hair with her left hand like a schoolgirl calling a boy for the first time, nervous and unsure of what to say. "Well, the invitation's open if you change your mind..."

"I know. I just have these people coming."

My mistake was deciding to go anyway. But you see, Grace was right. I *didn't* need to be alone on Thanksgiving. And since my family's gone and even the most anti-social of my friends goes home for the holidays, my only other option was to join the legions of losers, down-on-their-luck bowery bums, and other Edward Hopper extras at the Waffle House for the traditional Thanksgiving fare: scattered, smothered, and covered.

Grace and Jimmy met me on the porch, she with a hug and he with firm grip.

"Come on in here, Aleck; let's get that chill off you. Everybody's here but Jessi, and I expect her directly." She ushered Jimmy and me in like a hen nudging her chicks into the coop.

"Gracious, Aleck," she scolded as I took off my pea coat, "what have you been eating? You're all bone and hair."

"How you been keeping, son?" Jimmy asked, not giving me a chance to answer his wife. "You staying for the Tech / Georgia game this afternoon?"

"Is'at Aleck?" came a booming voice from the den. "I didn't think you was coming."

I looked at Grace and Jimmy as if they had spoken. "My ... uh ... friends had to cancel."

"That's what I figured," Grace returned with a smile. "Go in there and say 'hey' to Uncle Birch. We'll eat just as soon as Jessica gets here."

There was a fire burning in the den, and Uncle Birch sat with his bare feet propped on the hearth, smoking a pipe, and staring into space.

"I saw that picture you took in the paper today," he snapped.

Here we go, I thought as I entered the den and took a seat on the sofa. "You did, huh? What'd you think?" I knew the answer before I asked the question.

"Tell the truth, I didn't think too much about it at all." Birch made a face. "*PETA* [he pronounced the name as if it were something disgusting he found on his shoe] picketing the governor's mansion about eating turkeys on Thanksgiving."

"Well," I said, trying to ward off one of Birch's diatribes against the evils of the Animal Empire, "I guess they got a right to their opinion."

"Bah."

There are phrases that do things to people. Words that can turn an ordinarily sane man into a raving lunatic. "Tax break" is one such phrase. "Communist Manifesto" is another. For my father it was "Left-wing liberal" or "equal opportunity employer." Uncle Birch's phrase is "animal rights."

You see, Jessi's great-uncle Birtram, who at seventy-one is the oldest living member of the Collins family and the acting patriarch, has been steadily losing his mind for as long as anyone can remember. He doesn't rave. He doesn't forget anybody's name; quite the contrary, Birch Collins has the best memory of anyone I've ever known. He can remember the name of everyone he's ever met and can tell you to the minute when he met them, the last time he saw them, and the details of any event in between.

No, Birch's dementia takes the form of an irrational conspiracy theory. He believes, with a conviction bordering on the religious, that there is a conspiracy among the animal kingdom to overthrow humanity and rule the world. It began in the late sixties when in the midst of a raging mid-life crisis, Birch got hold of some bad acid while he was making out with a twenty-something political science major and listening to Pink Floyd's album *Ummagumma*. The acid kicked in just before Birch did, during track six, "Several Species of Small Furry Animals Gathered Together in a Cave and Grooving with a Pict," and Birch watched his partner transform into an epileptic snake with a she-wolf's head.

Since then he has done everything he can to stem the flow of this international conspiracy of the lesser species. In the early seventies, he lobbied to make George Orwell's *Animal Farm* required reading in all grades because it "shines the light of truth on what's *really* going on." The mid-eighties found him launching a grass-roots campaign of one against the comic strip *Bloom County* because it allegedly supported crossbreeding among the species by having "an obviously in-bred penguin marry a beautiful young hippie girl." He even credited himself with the strip's demise five years later.

It's no surprise, then, that Birch has been barely on speaking terms with his family since they became vegetarians.

Rather than respond to the "unneighborliness" of eating turkey on Thanksgiving, I sat before the fire, studying the den. Grace rarely lit more than one lamp, and the heavy curtains were usually drawn, giving the room a cozy kind of cave feeling. The stone fireplace took up most of the outside wall.

Above the fireplace hung the large Collins family portrait. The picture had been taken in front of the weeping willow in the backyard. Grace stood smiling shyly in the background with Jimmy on her right staring sternly into the camera and Birch on her left positively scowling (having decided, I suppose, that primitive animal worshippers were right and cameras really did capture the soul but uncertain whether or not this

played into the lower creature's hands). In the foreground sat
the two sisters, Jessi between her mother and father grinning
slyly at the cameraman with a come-hither twinkle in her eyes,
and her older sister, Leslie-Anne, between Birch and Grace
smirking mischievously.

I had taken the picture shortly after moving in with Jessi.
Grace wanted me posed between the two daughters, but the
camera was new, and I couldn't figure out the timer feature. If
you took the portrait out of its frame and looked closely at the
left-hand side, though, you could just see the edge of my right
sleeve in the negative space. To make up for my absence, Grace
had stuck a black and white five-by seven headshot into the
bottom right-hand corner of the larger picture.

Sitting proudly beneath the portrait on the right-hand side
of the mantle was the framed GED Leslie-Anne had received the
year before from Catagua Technical School. Across from this,
Grace had placed Jessi's Master's of Arts degree in sociology. I
smiled when I saw this, remembering the first day I had seen
her.

I met Jessica Belle Collins when we were both kicked out of
an introductory course on anthropological issues in post-
modern and contemporary feminist sociology. On the first day,
during a discussion on dating rituals, Jessi made the
unfortunate mistake of referring to her gender as "chicks."

"We do *not*," Dr. Malcomb coolly informed her slowly
cleaning his wire-rimmed glasses with a white handkerchief,
"refer to women as 'chicks.'"

Jessi looked down contritely. "I'm sorry," she said quietly,
"Broads, dames, skirts. Whatever."

I was the only one who laughed.

My reverie was interrupted, however, by the sound of a car
pulling into the driveway.

"That'll be Jessi." I rose from my seat.

Perhaps, I'd later tell myself, I should've actually *told* Jessi that I'd be joining them for Thanksgiving. I simply assumed her mother had cleared it with her beforehand. Of course, Grace may well have done just that, and then told her I declined. Either way, I'm sure she was just as surprised by my presence as I was by that of the skateboarder she brought with her.

The first thing you noticed about him was the three-inch strip of short, black hair extending from the forehead to the neck of his otherwise bald head and ending in a ponytail, which reached to the middle of his leather jacket. Then you noticed the metal chain connecting his left ear to his right ear by way of each nostril and his upper lip. Various other rings and bars and studs accented what was left of his face. He even had silver trinkets woven into his baby-blue goatee. I hated him immediately.

"My friend, Ratt," Jessi said by way of introduction as she removed her fur-lined coat revealing a woven halter top and a black pleated mini-skirt. Patent-leather Mary Janes over black knee-highs completed her outfit. "Ratt, this is Mom and Dad." She nodded towards Grace and Jimmy then motioned towards Birch emerging from the den. "That there's Uncle Birch. Uncle Birch, this is Ratt. He's going to eat with us tonight."

Birch glared at the prepubescent punk and slowly mouthed his name.

"That's Ratt with two t's," Jessi added reassuringly, "like the band, not like the rodent."

Birch would have none of it, though, two t's notwithstanding. He shook his head and snorted in disgust as he shuffled into the dining room, mumbling something about hell and handbaskets. Ratt said nothing.

That left all the introductions done but mine. There we stood in uncomfortable silence: me, my wife, and the prick. I could tell Jessi was uncomfortable, and even though I shouldn't have, I felt sorry for her.

However, I couldn't simply stand there smiling and pretend to be some friend of the family. I tried unsuccessfully to grin and be civil, but all I could do was mumble something incoherent and stick out my hand.

Ratt sucked on his whiskers, and grunted noncommittally, but otherwise said nothing. Jessi smiled at me as I slowly lowered my hand, and Grace ushered us into the dining room. I couldn't tell, though, if her smile came from gratitude, discomfort, or humor. Maybe all three.

"I hope you don't mind," Jessi murmured to her mother as they entered the dining room, "but he didn't really have anywhere else to go," she leaned in towards Grace's ear, "and I didn't think *he* would come." She nodded in my direction.

"That's fine, sweetheart," Grace said absently, glancing from her daughter to Ratt to me, "We can just pull up another chair."

I looked at the place settings on the small table, and felt briefly like an intruder. Grace had prepared a Thanksgiving dinner anticipating only the immediate family. Now I was here unexpectedly, and Jessi had seen fit to bring her friend. Watching Grace examine me and the boy, I could all but hear her silently calculating whether there was enough food or not.

I took a mental count of all assembled. There was Birch sitting at the head of the table and trying not to stare too openly at my wife's companion who had just taken the place beside him. Jimmy took the seat next to his uncle. I glanced at Jessi sitting to Ratt's left then at Grace retreating into the kitchen. I stood uncertainly behind the only other open seat not wanting to take Grace's spot.

"Here, Mr. Ratt," Grace emerged from the kitchen with a folding aluminum chair, "you can sit here next to me." Her face fell when she saw that Ratt was already sitting between her daughter and Uncle Birch. The young rodent merely continued to chew on his whiskers and said nothing, but Jessi's eyes widened.

"That's alright, Grace," I volunteered before Jessi could speak, "I don't mind sitting next to you."

It was Grace's turn to look disappointed, but only for a second. "Well aren't you just the sweetest thing." She patted my cheek and, after some quick shuffling of plates and silverware, placed the new chair to her right. Then she returned to the kitchen and brought out a little plate of sandwiches that she put beside Birch's place.

"Them my meat sammiches?" He asked.

"They are."

Birch lifted the top slice of bread off one of them and inspected the treasure within. "D'you remember to put the jelly on?"

"I didn't forget," Grace said, "but I didn't do it either. You know what the doctor said."

"Yeah I know what he said," Birch rose from his seat and went into the kitchen, "and I'll die and burn in hell before I listen to someone who donates money to the humane society."

Grace just shook her head in exasperation and continued setting out the food. Shortly we could hear the sounds of Birch shuffling through the garbage can, and then he emerged from the kitchen carrying a white aluminum can with the word "MEAT" printed on it in large square letters. He looked at all assembled, smiled, and held the can aloft as if it were the Holy Grail and he were Percival returning from the quest. He took his seat and set to work spreading a clear gelatinous substance from the can onto his sandwiches.

"The jelly's the best part," he informed us solemnly.

After Grace had placed the food on the table and taken her seat beside me, Jimmy looked at Birch and nodded. Birch bowed his head, and we all took hands (I noticed Birch cringe before taking the prick's hand).

"Our Heavenly Father," Birch prayed, "thank You for this bounteous food and all Your many blessings. Please help us to mend our ways, which are evil in Your holy sight, and help us to be better stewards of your creation. In Your name we pray. Amen."

We all repeated "Amen" and squeezed each other's hands.

"Well," Jimmy looked over the food spread out before him, "I reckon we can eat now."

That's when I realized that we weren't all here. Five place settings, and Grace hadn't planned on either Ratt or me attending.

"Where's Leslie-Anne?" I asked.

There was an uncomfortable silence.

"She won't be eating with us this year," Jimmy coolly informed me.

Birch cleared his throat and looked pointedly away, mumbling.

"She's eating with Denise's family this year," Grace added then slapped herself on the forehead. "Will you look at that? I forgot the main dish." She rose from her place and once again disappeared into the kitchen. She returned almost immediately, carrying a platter upon which sat a strange looking pinkish white loaf, and set it in the center of the table.

Birch regarded this addition with a crinkled face and a scowl. "What the hell is that?"

"You know good'n'well what that is." Grace again took her seat and flapped her napkin into her lap. "It's the turkey."

"The hell it is." Birch was struggling to keep his voice calm. "It's that damned turkey substitute. Where's the meat?"

"I've told you before, Birch, you don't have to eat the tofurkey. That's why I made you the sandwiches." Birch snorted in disgust, and Grace calmly dipped mashed potatoes on her plate, passed them to me, and turned to her husband. "Jimmy, please pass me the peas."

There was an awkward silence during dinner. I know that family gatherings often degenerate into silence as each member slowly understands that the time spent away between holidays has done nothing but increase the generational gap between himself and his relations. In fact, it's my firm belief that that's why we have so many football games on holidays; it keeps this realization at bay. No matter how far we've grown apart over the last year, we can still stare blindly at the television screen and cheer for the same team. However, this silence sprang not from distance but from its opposite, and Grace did not allow television in the dining room.

"How've you been?" Jessi murmured as she reached across me to get a second helping of food.

"Okay, I guess." I looked at the space between her leg and mine and wondered fleetingly if I could touch her bare knee. "You look nice."

"Thanks, wanna roll?"

"Uh ... sure, darlin'. Where?" I wondered fleetingly how we'd get away without offending anyone.

"Right here, silly." She smiled at me, and for a brief second, I was taking the family portrait again, madly in love, and a million miles away from nowhere.

"What?"

"Right here." She offered me a towel-covered basket with steam escaping. "A roll. Do you want one?"

"Oh! Yeah, yeah. Thanks."

She frowned at me, shook her head, and turned back to her plate.

Birch had not taken his eyes off Ratt since asking the blessing. At first the old man had tried his best to be discreet, glancing at his neighbor only when taking a bite of food and then quickly scanning the rest of the table. Gradually though, Birch became less and less surreptitious until now, he glared openly at the kid with a look of mixed disgust and curiosity. This attention was not going unnoticed by its object either. After a minute or so of this scrutiny, Ratt set his fork down and stared defiantly back at the old man.

"Dude, what's your problem?"

Birch jerked as if he'd been slapped. "Eh? You talking to me, sonny?"

"Yeah, man. Why you wanna keep staring at me? Didn't your mama tell you it was rude?"

Jessi patted his shoulder and murmured something into his ear.

"Listen, babe. I don't care if he *is* senile," he shook her off and looked again at Birch. "That don't make it right to stare."

"Well," Birch leaned closer to him. "You *do* have all that..." he waved his hand in the general vicinity of Ratt's face, "stuff stuck in yer face. If you dress y'self up like a circus freak and go paradin' down the street," Birch took a breath, "and don't charge nothin', people will stop and look."

"Birch," Grace said softly, "let it go."

"I'll be damned if I will!" Birch tossed his napkin on his plate and glared at his niece. "You may want to turn a blind eye to what's going on around here, but I won't."

"Not now, Birch," Jimmy kept his voice even but firm.

"Why not now? You two want to pretend there's nothin' goin' on, but I can't live thattaway. One daughter a damned anteater livin' with another woman like man and wife. What do you reckon they're doin'? Playin' tittly-winks?" The old man leveled a finger at Grace then moved it to Jimmy. "Y'all know how I feel about those shenanigans. I'm tellin' you, homer-sexuality is just a plot to thin our numbers for the revolution by keepin' folks from procreatin'. But don't nobody listen to me. No sir, I'm just ol' Barmy Birch, but you'll see.

"And you, missy," he turned his attention to Jessi, now. "You broke my heart; you know that? Now, there ain't no shame in leavin' a husband. If two people cain't get along, there's no point in livin' together. But shackin' up with someone while yer still married is beyond the pale." Jessi's face drained, and she put her hands in her lap.

"You're married?!" Ratt turned so quickly his chain flicked him in the right eye.

I cradled my chin on steepled arms and looked at my wife from the corner of my eyes. "So this is why you don't return my calls, huh?"

"You're married to *this* loser?!" Ratt's chain flicked him in the other eye as he turned sharply away from Jessi.

Birch continued. "As if that wa'nt enough, though, *this* is who you choose to share yer bed with." Birch waved a disdainful hand at Ratt. "A damned wannabe rodent. What're you tryin' to prove, boy? Why you wanna decorate y'self up like a goddamned porky-pine fer? And what kinda name is Ratt? Ain't you got any human decency? Any pride?"

"That's about enough, Birch!" Jimmy rose from the table and grabbed Birch's shirt. "These are guests in my house, and you will treat them as such!"

Birch looked from his nephew's hands to his face with an expression of pained betrayal. "You're takin' their side, Jimmy? Against your own blood?"

Jimmy released his uncle and took his seat with a sigh. "Jessi and Leslie-Anne are my blood,too, and their lives are their own."

Birch quietly rose from his seat and pushed it under the table. "Well," he said as he walked out of the dining room, "I should of expected as much from a couple of vegetarian collaborationists."

We sat around the table for several heartbeats before anyone said anything; finally, Grace broke the silence. "Well, would anyone like some rhubarb pie?"

"I appreciate it, Grace," I slid back from the table, "but I should probably be going. It's getting late."

Grace looked up at me from her seat then turned her attention to Jessi who was still sitting in her place and staring at her hands in her lap. "Are you sure, Aleck? I wish you'd stay."

I knew then that Grace had set this dinner up for me. She knew Leslie-Anne wouldn't be here tonight, and she still set five places. I looked down at her and knew that she had hoped that Jessi and I would reconcile, or maybe she'd been denying that anything at all was wrong. Probably both. Hope and denial are so frequently intertwined that one is often mistaken for the other.

I looked at Jessi again, then at Ratt sitting in my place. Grace may have wished for a reconciliation between her daughter and me, but I knew that it wasn't going to happen. That bird had flown.

"I should go." I folded my chair and leaned it against the wall. "I'm sorry."

"Wait a minute, Aleck." Jessi folded her napkin into her plate and pushed herself away from the table. "I'll walk you out."

"I'm sorry you had to find out like that," she said as we stood on the porch looking out at the overcast afternoon sky.

"So, do we get one lawyer or two?" I stood on the top step of the porch not looking at her.

"I don't want to talk about this right now." She folded her arms across her chest and stood next to me. "Talk about something else."

"How long has it been going on?" I looked at the space between the porch and my car and pulled a crumpled pack of cigarettes from my pocket.

"Since July."

"Why?" It was all I could think of to say. "He's what? Twelve?"

"He's twenty-four, and I don't know why," I could feel her looking at me. "Maybe because he makes me feel *real* for the first time in my life. Everyone I know, except for Uncle Birch, goes through life like a zombie. They don't act; they react, and sometimes not even that. Even you."

"Oh, really?"

Her voice became more animated now. "Yes, you especially. You're so busy looking at the world through your camera lens that you forget to actually interact with it. Everything's a composition for you. Something to be studied, observed, and then rearranged into your idea of order." She raised her hands as if to illustrate a point, and let them fall uselessly by her side with a sigh.

"I don't know," she continued. "Maybe it's a safety mechanism for you or something. Like if you don't interact with the world, it can't hurt you. If you organize it yourself, it can't control you. You always keep yourself aloof, Aleck, apart from everyone around you, and your were holding me apart right along with you. Maybe, I just wanted to be a part of life. I was tired of being just a picture for you to appreciate."

I shook out a cigarette and tapped it on my palm, then lit it. I couldn't think of anything to say, so I stood there for a minute, thinking about the family portrait. How I'd been unable to make it into the big picture, so I'd been stuck in later in black and white.

"Ratt treats me like a person. We *do* things just for the hell of it. When I met him, he was racing shopping carts with his friends down the embankments behind Kroger. I didn't know him from Adam when he asked me to climb into his buggy because he needed someone to steer. We spent three hours just pushing each other downhill in the shopping carts. Just because it was fun. When was the last time you and I did anything just for fun? He's good for me, Aleck. I'm good for him, too."

We stood in silence for a minute, and I realized that though I had lived with my wife for years, I never knew her, but she understood me perfectly.

"What're you going to do now? Where are you going?" She asked, taking my cigarette from me and pulling a drag off it before stomping it out on the porch.

"I don't know. I'll probably go to the Waffle House and then out to the studio. I still have some frames to fix for Saturday's paper."

I looked at her and smiled. "I'll be fine."

Jessi shook her head and went back in.

I stood on the Collins' porch for a minute, thinking about what Jessi had said. Like so many of her explanations, her words seemed crystal clear as she spoke, but once she left me alone, they began to grow foggy and unfocused, leaving only the sensation that Jessi had a point, whether I could remember it or not. As I turned to go, I could hear the sounds of Jessi and her mother cleaning up after the aborted dinner while Jimmy, Ratt, and Birch cheered the Bulldogs on in the den.

Sermon

Christ looked upon
The multitudes
And smiled,
Saying:

Blessed are the poor
In spirit
For theirs is
The Kingdom of Heaven.

Blessed are those
Who mourn
For they shall
Be comforted.

Blessed are the meek
For they shall inherit
The Earth.

And James the Greater
Cried unto Christ
Saying:
"Master, we hunger."

And James the Lesser
Cried unto Christ
Saying:
"Master, we thirst."

And the Lord replied:

Blessed are those
That do hunger

And thirst
For they shall
Be filled.

And so saying
He took forth
A fish;
He took forth a loaf
And did feed the multitudes
Upon them.
He drew forth water
And did turn it to wine.

There was much rejoicing.

Blessed are the merciful
For they shall
Obtain mercy.

Blessed are the pure

And Thomas did cry out
Saying:
"Master,
Are You sure it's the meek
Who'll inherit
And not the poor?"

And the Lord did reply
Yes,
I'm quite sure.

Blessed are the pure

And Luke said unto the Lord:
"Master,

Couldst thou
Speak up?
I didn't quite catch
The last bit."

Blessed are the pure
In heart

And James the Lesser asked:
"O, Master,
May I go
To relieve myself?
Thy wine works quick."

For they shall see God.

And Peter called
To the Lord
Saying:
"Master,
Should we
Be taking notes?"

And Mark did ask:
"Will this be on a test?"

And there was
Wailing
And gnashing of teeth.

Blessed are the persecuted
For theirs is
The Kingdom of Heaven.

"I thought,"
Replied Thomas,

"The poor had the Kingdom of Heaven."

And Judas Iscariot
Did call out
Saying:
"I won't share Heaven
With some bum,
O Lord.
Surely there has been
Some mistake?"

And Lo, the Philistines came
And requested
The Lord's
Lesson plans.

And the Romans
And the Elders
Did appear

Requesting
Alternate plans
For students with differing
Learning styles.

James returned
From the privies
And left his hall pass.

Judas called
His mother's lawyer
For advice.

And the Lord
Cried out:

My God
My God
Why hast Thou
Forsaken me?

Here ends the Lesson.

Gods for Sale, Cheap

"Finney, Moody, Keble, and Hare: Spiritual Designers; may I help you?"

"Oh I hope so. You see I'm quite at a loss."

"I'm sorry to hear that. How may I be of assistance, sir?"

"My wife says I need to find religion."

"Very good, sir. Any particular religion? We're running a special this week on Zoroastrianism."

"Oh, really? You have a religion that worships Zorro?"

"Not as such, no. Zoroastrians believe the universe is created by one all-powerful and benevolent god named Ahura Mazda..."

"So they worship marginalized Japanese cars?"

"No, sir. As a point of fact, the car company is named after the god."

"Why?"

"Why what, sir?"

"Why is the company named after the god?"

"I'm sure I don't know, sir."

"Is the car company Zoroastrian?"

"One assumes not, sir."

"I certainly hope not. They're not like Scientologists, right? They don't keep an office in all the car dealerships waiting for this Mazda fellow to come back and improve the stock quotes do they?"

"I do not believe that is the case, sir."

"Well, tell me more about this Zoroastrianism, but I must tell you, so far I am not impressed."

"Well, opposing Mazda is the personification of evil."

"Chrysler?"

"No. Angra Mainyu, actually."

"Angry Man? Really?"

"It means 'destructive spirit.'"

"How original."

"Indeed. Zoroastrians believe that as worshippers of Mazda, they must actively demonstrate good thoughts, words, and deeds in order to help their god keep the forces of destruction at bay. In the end, Mazda will defeat Mainyu and bring about the end of time. After which the world will be remade into a paradise and all the dead will rise to be brought back into oneness with Mazda."

"Let me get this straight, then. The universe is ruled by one all-powerful god who wants us to be good and who is engaged in a struggle with the living representative of evil and chaos. At the end of the world, evil is banished and the righteous go to a kind of paradise for eternity."

"That's about the shape of it, yes. It's quite a nice little religion actually. We're running a special on it, as I mentioned. Only a five percent annual tithing."

"It seems a bit run-of-the-mill."

"Well, it has been an influence on quite a few of our other religions."

"You don't say? Look, don't you have anything a bit off the beaten track?"

"We do have the Seventh Day Adventists."

"No. I'm looking for something a little more, I don't know, *different*. You know what I mean?"

"I could set you up with some Juddhism."

"I'm familiar with Judaism, thank you. I'm not completely uninformed you know."

"No. Juddhism; it's fairly new. It's a blend of Judaism and Buddhism. Quite a bit of meditating. Lot of the young people going out for that one."

"Not interested."

"Well, there is one other I could show you."

"How much ritual is involved? I'm not one for getting up early on the weekends."

"There is quite a bit of ritual involved, I'm afraid, but it's mostly late at night."

"Go on."

"I have to admit now the god, well gods, don't play much of a role in the day-to-day workings of the world."

"A bit hands-off, eh? That's not a problem. I never have been one for micromanaging deities."

"These are certainly not that. Most of them are dead."

"Really? Doesn't seem much of a point in worshipping them; does it? I mean, fat lot of good a dead god can do, right?"

"Ask Nietzsche. It doesn't really apply to these gods, though. They communicate with their followers through dreams."

"Now what the devil does that mean? Are they dead or aren't they?"

"They *are* dead, but they are also ... dreaming."

"Right, you said that. It doesn't make sense."

"Think of it as a religious mystery then, like virgin births, flaming bushes, and sacred cows."

"Why on earth would I pay good money to participate in a religion that doesn't make sense?"

"Many do, sir. In this case, though, it doesn't have to make sense; there are fringe benefits that don't necessarily come with the other religions."

"Such as?"

"Well, provided you make the right sacrifices, show the proper respect, and so on, the gods of R'lyeh (that's their city) promise to deliver unto you riches and fortune beyond your own dreaming."

"Oh, they promise, do they?"

"Promise and deliver, sir. Ever been to Innsmouth, Massachusetts? Ask them. Never had such good fishing before they took up the faith."

"Hmmm. Maybe I ought to think about it first."

"Don't think long, sir. We have a special on this one, too, but it ends soon."

"How soon?"

"Tomorrow, next week. Hard to say. Whenever the stars are right."

"Alright, then. I guess I'll take it."

"Are you sure?"

"I guess so."

"You need to be a bit more certain than that. This is your spiritual livelihood we're talking about."

"Okay, then I'm sure. I'm positive. I'm as certain of this as I am of anything else. How much? Another five percent discount on tithing? Four percent?"

"Oh no, sir, there's no monthly plan for this one. Just one single payment."

"How much then? I'm a bit strapped for cash at the moment."

"Sir, the Esoteric Order only demands a service of you."

"What kind of service?"

"Oh you have choices. That's one of the top selling points of this one. Do you have any daughters?"

"No, I'm afraid not."

"No matter, sons?"

"I have no children."

"I see. Well you could have married one or two of them off to the Deep Ones, kind of the high priests of the Order, but ..."

"I have a nephew I'm not too fond of. Could we use him?"

"I'm afraid they demand a direct blood tie. So we're left with Sanity or Soul, which do you use the least?"

"I'm afraid I don't understand."

"You can give the Deep Ones your sanity or your soul. Whichever one you don't need. They're not that picky."

"Well, what is the use of being rich if you're not sane enough to enjoy it?"

"Soul it is then. So, we have one submission to the Esoteric Order of Dagon, Cthullhu sect. Soul to be delivered according to ancient rituals upon conclusion of business. Will this be billed or credit?"

"I thought you said the Order required a service. No money."

"That is true. But there is a minor handling fee for us, thirteen dollars is all. Billed or credit?"

"Credit I guess. Do you take VISA?"

"American Express, actually."

Misdirection

"We do what we do because of who we are. If we did otherwise, we would not be ourselves." - Neil Gaiman

I.

You know, sometimes, when I get in a funk, I really hate my life. I mean I get to thinking about the routine, you know. How I'm not really doing nothing with myself. I get this way especially late at night when I'm sitting in the corner of some Southside dive after a hard day pounding the pavement, helping the helpless. I just sulk there in the darkness nursing a whiskey brooding on my go-nowhere life.

Mornings are worse, though, when I crawl out from under my rock after the alcohol has absorbed all the water from my system and my body's instant pudding and my head feels like the sun being crammed into Mars.

Ziggy, I think to myself, *you've got to find yourself another line of work.*

I'm in what you might call a service industry. I take up for the downtrodden and the defenseless, for a nominal fee, mind you (I may live in a rat hole, but I still got bills). Like this morning, for instance, I'd been out to the Bucket O'Blood last night, drowning my sorrows in a bit of Ol'Scratch, and I wake up somewhere between my bedroom and the john lying in a pool of my own creation with this ringing in my head that just won't quit. After a while, I realize that the ringing isn't in my head but under it. I sit up groggily and pat down my bile-sodden shirt until I find my cell phone.

"McAlistair here," I mumble into the speaker trying not to breathe, "Whaddaya want?"

The last voice anybody wants to hear first thing in the morning when he's fighting off a hangover is his boss. Well, I guess that's an exaggeration; the last voice anybody really wants to hear first thing in the morning when he's fighting off a hangover is the Voice of God reading His Final Judgment, but that's six of one, half dozen of the other if you ask me.

"Ah, Mr. McAlistair," Mr. Nalson's voice always sounds measured and calm, like nothing in the world can surprise him. It's always crystal clear, too, despite the faint buzzing on his end of the line. "I'm glad to see you're up. Long night?"

"You might say that," I try to stand slowly and brush the dried vomit, beer, and crumbs from my shirt. Whenever I talk to Lucky Nalson, it's like he's in the room with me even if he's in the other hemisphere. I feel vaguely ashamed and even dirtier than usual.

"Well, get yourself cleaned up, then, and fetch Mr. Griffin, I've got some work for you two this morning."

II.

It don't take me but thirteen minutes to shower, shave, and get out the door on any given day. You see back in the service, we had to snap to real quick, but I've gotten lax since joining the civvie world, and I can't get going quite as quick as I used to. Be that as it may, this morning, I'm cleaned up in a new pair of jeans and a reasonably clean Hawaiian shirt, and I'm cranking up the van before you can scratch.

Hode Griffin's my partner. Work partner, mind you. I don't get into that freaky stuff. Me and Griff's strictly business, you know. He won't even drink with me after work. Five o'clock rolls around, and we just head off into the sunset ... except in different directions, of course.

Overall, Griff looks like the product of an unfortunate union between Jimmy Durante and a troll. He's got the largest nose this side of Paradise, and he's about six feet tall. He's also got this weird discolored skin, blue-grey like he's either been buried in ash or held under water too long. He always wears this dark brown duffel coat over a pair of faded Oshkosh B'gosh overalls and a yellowing "Kool-Aid" t-shirt. Except for a couple tufts of grey hair growing out his ears, he's completely bald. He must be going blind, too; he wears these thick glasses because he claims he has poor day vision, but at night he can see like a hawk.

He's already waiting on me when I pull into his alley, squinting through the smoke of those sulphur-smelling cigars he's always puffing on.

"For Chrissakes, Griff," I scowl and fan his smoke back in his face as he climbs into the van, "if you're gonna ride with me, have the fucking decency to put that damned stinkweed out."

Griff manages to crawl into the passenger seat and stubs his cigar out on the sole of his left work boot. Yellow ash falls onto the floorboard, but he smears it into the carpet with his right foot and grunts at me. "You look like shit, Ziggy. Fall asleep in your own puke again?" Griff's gravelly voice rattles some people, but I find it oddly comforting. It reminds me of my dad.

"Shut the fuck up and lemme drive." Griff obliges me and just chews on his cigar stub until we get to the diner.

III.

Lucky loves this god-forsaken place. He says it's got that "down-home" feeling. Down-trodden's more like it. Now, I admit, Hell's Ditch has some little claim to fame since it's one of the last family-owned-and-run diners left in this world of Waffle and Huddle Houses. What's even more amazing is that it could stay in business. The owner must've made some kinda deal with either the health department or the devil as filthy as it is. But the boss likes it, so I guess that means I got to also ... or at least keep my opinions about it to myself.

Lucky's nowhere to be seen when we walk into the diner. He never is. He kind of runs this business on the side. You see, Lucky works for Allen Fodder, maybe you've heard of him. Al's kinda like a judge for the private sector. "Lord of the Gallows" I think they call him. I've only ever seen him once, but that was enough.

He's much taller than Lucky with a predilection for bluish-grey suits and wide-brimmed hats. He wears this wicked looking patch over one of his eyes (word has it, he lost the eye in a bet over a fucking glass of wine), and his remaining eye is the brightest shade of yellow I've ever seen.

Anyway, Lucky doesn't wanna get on Al's bad side, and I suspect Al'd be pretty upset with the idea of Lucky's moonlighting, so he has to sneak out of his basement office and get his secretary to cover for him whenever he gets a commission for me and Griff. As a result, he's almost always late for our meetings.

Griff, chewing on the still smoldering cigar stub, lopes to the back and slides into the booth next to the bathrooms as Bob, the greasy, over-weight cook, glares at him over a pot of chili.

"Hey, buddy," he growls in the deep drawl predominant in these parts, "I done told you before, you cain't be smoking in this here establishment."

Griff holds up his unlit stub without looking at the man. The cook glares again at my companion, then nonchalantly flicks his own cigar ash on the floor before stirring the chili. "Jesus," Griff mumbles as I slide in beside him, "suddenly everybody's a friggin' health nut."

The bench is amazingly inadequate for both me and Griff, and we're practically sitting in each other's laps like two queer peas in a pod while a perfectly good bench goes empty across from us. Looking over my shoulder at the entrance, I silently curse Lucky's name. He does this to me every time. I feel like a moron sitting here facing the wall. My dad survived twenty years walking a Chicago beat, taking no shit from nobody, only to have a cap popped in his ass, facing the wall at McGillicuddy's bar one night after his shift. Now here I am with just as many enemies as him, if not more, with my back to the door and my ass in the wind. "Where the fuck is that creepy son of a bitch?" I ask still watching the front.

"Now, Siegfried, is that any way to talk about the man who has done so much for you?" The voice comes from behind me, so I turn back and find Lucky sitting across from us, daintily wiping a ring of water with his handkerchief.

"Dammit, Boss, you know I hate it when you do that." I slide down and slouch uncomfortably on the bench as Bertha the waitress, a large misshapen mass of a woman, puts down three glasses of iced water and walks off before we can place an order.

Lucky just tucks his handkerchief back in the breast pocket of his dark grey pinstriped suit and smiles serenely at me. He's a gaunt man, Lucky is. When he smiles, his mouth seems to take up the better part of his face, like the Grinch, and his beady little red eyes beam from under the fiery hair hanging over his pale brow. From inside his jacket, he produces a sealed envelope with my name written in pristine script across the front and places it on the table.

"I don't have much time, gentlemen, so I'll get right to the point." he slides the envelope to me. "Inside that envelope, you'll find the name and address of a man who took something of value some time ago from our client, a Mister Albert Rich, and we've been asked to intercede on the matter."

I open the envelope, and a business card falls out:

William Dair
Benchmark Financial Services
Reclamations Department

On the back is written Mr. Dair's address:

1314 Ash Lane
Owen, Georgia

"A repo man, boss?" I shake my head, put the envelope back on the table, my name up, and sip my water. "What are we, slumming now?"

"We go where the money is, Mr. McAlistair." Lucky strikes a match on his palm and holds it to the envelope. "And today, the money is with Messieurs Dair and Rich."

I watch my name crinkle up and blacken as Lucky speaks, then Griff, who's been sitting there like a bump on a log this whole time, chimes in with his two cents. "I got no problem with that, boss." He tries to relight his cigar on the envelope, but I pour water on the flame before he can get it to his stub. "How y'want the job done?" Griff glares at me as I begin sopping up the water with our napkins.

"I simply wish you two to have a polite word with Mr. Dair. Explain to him that Mr. Rich wants his property back. Dair is a reasonable and wise man; I'm sure he'll be as helpful as it's in his power to be."

"And if he isn't?" Griff leans a little towards Lucky.

"Offer him an out, and if he refuses, enjoy yourselves." Lucky reaches again into his jacket and removes a wallet-sized photo flip album and a roll of bills. He pulls a twenty off the top and places it precisely in the center of the table, amidst the water, slushy ash, burned envelope, and pulpy napkin. He then hands the album and the rest of the money to me. "Now you're on my clock; get to work, boys. I've got to get back and chain myself to the desk again before that one-eyed son of a frost giant misses me."

We get up to leave, and Lucky calls to us as we reach the door. "Oh, and boys?"

We look back.

"Whatever you do, don't hurt the merchandise."

IV.

As soon as we pull out of Hell's Ditch, Griff turns to me and starts talking around his cigar. "So you gonna tell me about it, or am I gonna have to play twenty questions?"

"What're you jawing about?" I cut off a tractor-trailer as I pull onto the road and head into town. I step on the gas, oblivious to the truck's blaring horn behind me.

"Yer in a mood."

"A mood, Griff?"

"A mood. Somethin's botherin' you an' I wanna know what it is." Griff chews thoughtfully on his cigar stub.

"How's it any of your business, Griff? My moods are my own."

"It's my business because your mood swings can screw up our work. My work. I wanna get paid, too, you know." He presses the dashboard cigarette lighter.

I cut my eyes towards his hands on the lighter. "Please don't light that thing in here. I'm begging you."

"I'll roll the window down," he begins to crank the window handle, and an earsplitting creak comes out of his door. "That's another thing, since when do you care if I smoke in the truck or not?"

"It just bugs me, that's all. I'm tired of smelling like fire, brimstone, and shit every time I come home from work."

"Well," he pulls out the lighter and touches it to the end of his cigar, "I got news for you; it ain't the cigar doing that. It's the work."

"Well, maybe I'm tired of the work." I slow down, and the truck behind me renews its honking and rides my ass.

"Ah," Griff dismisses my complaint with a wave of his hand. "It's just a means to an end, my brother. A means to an end."

"What end, Griff?" I press the brakes some more, and the truck tries to pass me on a hill but almost collides with a station wagon coming the other way. I smile cheerlessly as the driver moves in behind me again. "This is what we do. It's what we've always done, and it's what we probably always will do."

"Lucky's not doing it anymore."

"Don't kid yourself. He does the same thing for Fodder that we do for him, just on a grander scale."

"Well, that's progress right there." Griff flicks yellow ash out his window and looks at me. "One day, we'll do it on a grander scale, too. One day we'll have Lucky's power. He said so hisself when we started. If we just play the game."

"We'll never see that power. We'll never see a grander scale." Though we're on a straightaway, I turn on my right blinker and slam on the breaks again. "Lucky invented the fucking game. He makes the rules; we follow'em."

"Nah," Griff shakes his head, "you're just hung over is all. Lucky wouldn't gyp us."

"Oh, give me a break. 'Wouldn't gyp us.' Lucky Nalson invented the fucking gyp. He taught P. T. Barnum everything he knew. He created Three Card Monte. He sold the first piece of beachfront property in Arizona. Wouldn't gyp us, my ass." The truck tries again to pass me, and I press the gas pedal to match his speed.

"We're too valuable to him." Griff reaches into the front pocket of his overalls and takes out the knife Lucky gave him for Christmas last year. It's a switchblade with a mistletoe handle. "Who else'd do his work for him?" He waves the shiv at me like it's proof of our value to Lucky.

"Look around, Griff. Any of these people could do our jobs. If we didn't do it, somebody else'd just come along and do it for us."

Griff just waves his hand at me and stares out the window with a disgusted grunt and begins a futile attempt to clean his fingernails with the knife. I finally let the truck pass, and we ride for the next few minutes in silence.

V.

Griff has this heavy silence, you know what I mean? For all his salt-of-the-earth gruffness, the little troll is too fucking sensitive, man. I mean, he can get his feelings hurt over nothing, and when he does, that little bastard will sulk like nobody's business. He stares away from you, focuses on the horizon, and just stares. His silence weighs you down like no amount of yelling and nagging and bitching can. It just settles there between you, and he never acknowledges it.

I don't know how long Griff can take it. The longest I've ever borne his silence was the time I made some off-hand remark comparing his Kool-Aid Man t-shirt and the shape of Griff's backside. He didn't speak for three days until I finally broke down and apologized. I spent the next week reassuring him that his ass wasn't too big, but he never really believed me. He wears that fucking duffel coat all year long now.

After we've been driving for about half an hour, I finally break the silence. "Look, I'm just tired of broken promises is all." Griff turns to look at me but still says nothing. "We were promised a future, and we haven't gotten it. I've been doing the same thing, day after day, year after year since I don't know when, and I'm just getting sick of it. I'm tired of looking forward to something and having it pulled out from under my feet. You know what I'm saying?"

Griff grunts noncommittally.

"Like the Y2K thing."

"Aw jeez," Griff rolls his eyes, "here we go again. Ziggy, ain't that dog dead yet?"

"It was a good idea, Griff. You know it was."

"If you say so."

Couple three years ago, everybody was freaking out about the coming millennium, like we'd never seen one before. Last time it was a plague or something that was gonna wipe us all out; this time it was computers. Apparently, the machines couldn't handle dates very well, and everything was supposed to shut down and freeze up on New Year's Day, 2000 A.D. Anyway, it was supposed to be this big disaster, a regular post-apocalyptic Mel Gibson movie complete with ravaging hordes of downwardly mobile city-dwellers killing each other off for food, shelter, and sex.

Well, Owen isn't large, but it is, technically speaking, a city, and it is right down the highway from Atlanta, so I figured we'd be seeing some of this ravaging action ourselves. I also figured that we'd be out of jobs, seeing as the local populace would be doing Lucky's job for him for free. So I worked out this masterful security system for me and my nearest and dearest. Well, Griff.

The beauty of this system was its stunning simplicity. It was basically a system of signals and countersignals, only streamlined. You see, the problem with most password systems is that they have to be changed fairly frequently. Not so with mine. I based my system on the number thirteen. Whenever someone knocked on my door, I'd give a number, and the countersignal would be whatever number would add up to thirteen. Griff and I practiced for weeks before the dreaded day.

"Eight," I'd say.

"Christ on a Cross, Ziggy."

"Eight."

"Come on. Lemme in dammit"

"Look, Griff, what if this was the real thing? How would I know it's you?"

Putrid yellow smoke would waft in under the door.

"Very funny. Eight."

"Alright already. Five. Are you happy now?"

But the four horsemen stayed home, and Ragnarok never came. The only thing that happened was the city hall lights went out precisely at midnight on New Year's Eve, but they go out precisely at midnight every night. I tried to keep up the practice, but it lost its magic when the computers kept working and life went on as normal.

Griff brings me out of my reverie by snapping his blade shut and turning to me. "Look," he says, "I ain't sayin' our job's a bed'o'roses, by any means. All I'm sayin' is it could be worse. What would we be without it?"

"Cleaner?"

"No." Griff points his stubby finger at me. "You'd be an unemployed alcoholic on skid row, and I'd be out in the street living behind a dumpster or something."

I look at him but say nothing.

"And we'd both be broke. What about that roll of bills Lucky gave us? Huh?" Griff smiles triumphantly. "Where we gonna get that kinda dough just for puttin' the fear o'God into some mope?"

"In a board game, maybe?" With one hand on the wheel, I reach into my pocket and toss him the roll. Griff's smile falls as he pulls the top two twenties from the roll. Underneath is a roll of light green bills sporting a stylized locomotive in the top right corner and a geometric house in the lower left. I turn left onto Ash Lane. There's only one driveway.

"The only thing keeping us here, Griff," I say as I pull onto the curb in front of the house, "is fear of what Lucky'd do if we stopped. We were promised, wealth, power, and principalities. We'll be lucky to be janitors of Powers and Principalities. Now put on your game face; we're here."

VI.

There's a wooden sign by the driveway. "Welcome to the Broad Gleaming Ringhorn," it says, "Please Keep off the Grass." I fucking hate people who name their houses. It's so pretentious, like they think they're gods or something. Who cares if it's got a silver roof and two gold pillars supporting the threshold? It's still not much of a house. For one thing, it's all one level and made of wooden logs like some kind of big frontier cabin; they can't even afford vinyl siding. It sits along the right side of the yard and parallel to it is another long wooden building with two cars in it. I smile to myself wondering what kind of idiots don't think to attach the garage to the rest of the house. At the head of the yard, he's built a kind of garden shed out of what must've been the leftover logs from the house and garage. He could've saved a lot of money if he'd forgotten about the silver and gold and built it all as one structure. He could've really had something to be proud of, but who am I to judge?

When we reach the door, I pull the cord for the door chime while Griff raps loudly on the brass knocker. Presently, the door is answered by the most beautiful man I've ever seen. Now I'm about as straight as they come; I'm all about the ladies. It's just that "beautiful" is the only word to adequately describe William Dair.

He stands a little taller than me, and even though he is pale of skin, this isn't a flaw since it accents his clothing perfectly. He's wearing this double-breasted white suit (which he fills out perfectly: not a wrinkle or a stretched seam anywhere) with a silver tie and golden pin. His most striking feature, though, is his face. His long hair is so white it gleams like the roof of his house, and underneath his bangs, his eyes are ice-blue and piercing. He smiles when he opens the door, and this calming feeling of gentle peace emanates from him. I hate him immediately.

"Good morning," he says, "May I help you?"

Suddenly I'm all professional. As much as I bitch about this job, I'm a natural at it. I really am. "Mr. Dair?"

"Yes?"

Griff stands slightly behind me and glares at him, trying to throw him off kilter, but Dair is the picture of serene congeniality.

"Mr. William Dair?" I ask, just to be sure. There could be more than one Dair here, you know.

"Yes?" Not even a hint of irritation. This guy is good. Griff quietly growls, but Dair seems not to notice.

"Bill?" A woman's voice comes from within. "Who is it?"

"Nobody, Nan." He speaks over his shoulder. "Just a couple of guys."

"What do they want?" She, at least, seems nervous.

"That's what I'm trying to find out, honey." He turns back to us. "What can I do for you fellows?"

"Rich sent us," Griff growls from behind me.

"Excuse me?" Dair's smile grows broader.

"Albert Rich." I stand up a little straighter and look Bill Dair right in the eye. "You took something very valuable from him some time ago, and he wants it back." I smile back at him.

"I'm afraid you boys are mistaken. I've taken nothing from Rich that didn't willingly part with him first." Dair steps onto his doorstep and tries to maneuver himself past us. "Now if you'll excuse me, I have to get to work. Please relay my condolences to Mr. Rich for his loss, but this envoy has been in vain."

I put my hand against the wall, blocking his path. "I'm afraid I can't do that, Mr. Dair. You see my instructions were very explicit."

VII.

Griff positions himself behind Dair, nonchalantly draws his knife, and once again begins cleaning his nails, smiling the whole time.

"Look, Bill," I move my hand to rest gently on his shoulder. Dair simply looks patiently into my face. "I don't want to do anything we'll both regret on later reflection. You see, I've found myself in a crisis of faith today."

"Weeping Jesus on Calvary," Griff sighs. "Give the poor man a break, will you? Just rough him up and move on."

I ignore him and look plaintively at Dair.

"Lately, my life has slipped into a direction I'm not sure I want it to go. I'm concerned about my future and afraid I don't really have one in my present circumstances."

Dair smiles and gently removes my hand from his shoulder. "Mr. McAlistair," he says gently. It's not until later that I wonder how he knew my name. "I believe I understand perfectly. We've all been through this before, and your answer is obvious."

"Would you two like to lie on a couch or somethin'?" Griff is tapping his foot impatiently and rubbing the mistletoe hilt of his knife. "I mean, I got nuthin' but time, here."

"I'm glad you understand, Mr. Dair. Truly, I am." I shoot Griff an irritated glance and continue. "We find ourselves in a seemingly hopeless situation. We've been tasked with retrieving Mr. Rich's property. Clearly, you're unwilling to assist. And honestly, who can blame you? I'm sure Nan is a beautiful woman, a loving wife, and loyal friend." Dair winces ever so slightly at the sound of his wife's name on my tongue. "Fortunately, I have been authorized to give you an out."

I've finally caught him off guard. I told you; I'm a natural at this job. For the first time since answering the door, Bill Dair blinks. "An out?" he asks. "What kind of an out?"

Griff catches up with me and smiles. I pull the photo album from my jacket pocket and flip it open. A chain of pictures unfolds, depicting women of all shapes and shades. "Pick one, and she's yours." My smile turns into a leer.

Dair's smile turns cold, and he stares daggers at me. "Not interested."

"I tell you what," I tuck the chain of pictures into Dair's breast pocket. "You drive a hard bargain, and I shouldn't do this; I really shouldn't, but go ahead and pick two. One for the weekends."

"I think the two of you should leave now. Obviously, your employer failed to inform you who I am, and I'll give you the benefit of a doubt."

Griff chuckles menacingly behind Dair. "Oh no, Bill. I know exactly who you are."

"I tell you what," My smile fades, and I look almost sadly into Dair's eyes. "As I said, I'm concerned about my life's misdirection, and instead of risking my own peace of mind, I'd rather let you consider our offer." I pat Dair reassuringly on his shoulder. "Why don't we come back in about an hour, hmm? Please have Mr. Rich's property packed and ready to go."

VIII.

It doesn't happen often, but I can be taken by surprise sometimes, and Dair's right hook into my jaw certainly does that. I never figured him for a southpaw. As my head whips around, something snaps. I understand who I am and what I do, and I slide comfortably back into my place in the world.

Yeah, the benefits suck, I think as I rub my jaw and glare coldly into Bill Dair's face, *but enjoyment has to count for something. After all, if you can't take pride in your own handiwork, what have you got?*

I shake off the pain as Griff grabs my assailant from behind and places the blade of his shiv ever so tenderly upon Dair's neck. "You shouldn't oughta done that to Ziggy." He whispers into Dair's right ear. "He don't like bein' hit."

I say nothing as I knee Dair's groin. He doesn't seem to react.

"Y'see," Griff continues, "His dad used to hit him as a kid."

I throw a punch into Dair's gut. Again, no reaction.

"So he walked into a bar one night and blew his ol' man's head clean off."

I go berserk, kicking, punching, slapping. I even bite his nose at one point and spit in his ear. Dair never so much as flinches.

"You don't wanna know what he did with the body."

"Bill, dear? What's going on?" A very fetching blonde stands just inside the doorway, clutching her dressing gown at her neck. I can see why Rich desires her so. While she's not as beautiful as Al Fodder's wife, Brigit, she's certainly a close second.

"Go back in the house. Now." Dair's voice is shaking with anger and fear, revealing his weakness.

"But Bal-"

"Dammit, Nanna! Go inside! Put the bar on the door and hide!" Dair is really scared now. Not because of what we can do to him. (Truth be told, I don't think there's much we can do to someone who apparently doesn't care about pain). No, Dair fears what we'll do to his wife.

"You needn't worry about the missus, Bill." I pat his silver hair reassuringly. Griff continues to hold him as I move to the door and try the latch. It won't budge. Bitch must've barred the door like he told her. I speak over my shoulder, "We've been instructed to leave her unharmed." I smile at the door and imagine the iron bar holding it in place. "You, however," I hear Griff snicker as I return to face our quarry. "Well, our employer gave us strict instructions to enjoy ourselves. I've had my fun, so now it's Griff's turn."

Griff laughs like a boy turned loose from school early, and presses his knife deeper into Dair's flesh. "I like this knife a lot, y'know. It's got craftsmanship. Not many people care about craftsmanship no more. Most things don't work like they're s'posed to, but this knife," Griff turns Dair around to face him. "This knife works. Lucky had it made for just this kind of situation."

For the second time, Dair is caught off guard. His eyes open wide, and his jaw drops. "Loki?"

Griff giggles like a schoolgirl as he drives the knife deep into Bill Dair's left eye. Then, because Griff has such an attraction for the symmetrical, he plunges the blade into Bill Dair's right eye. Dair doesn't react in the least as Griff removes the knife and wipes his finger across the blade to remove the clear sticky fluid. "You gotta take care of a blade like this. Don't want it to rust or nothin'." Griff sticks his finger in his mouth and licks it clean. "The jelly's the best part."

When Dair still makes no reaction, Griff gets frustrated. "Well, damn," he whines, "it's no fun playin' if yer not gonna act right." Then he plunges the knife into Dair's heart and almost goes through his spine. When he removes his arm from Dair's chest cavity, the body falls to the doorstep, face down and quite dead. Bill Dair never utters so much as a whimper.

IX

Griff uses the tail of his shirt to wipe Dair's blood from the switchblade.

I look disdainfully at his stained t-shirt. It looks like the Kool-Aid man wet himself. "What, you're not going to eat that, too?"

"Nah," he makes a face. "Too much iron makes my mouth taste funny. So what do we do now? Fetch the girl?"

"Don't think so." I point to the door. "She's barred us out, remember? I don't believe the two of us have the power to move an iron bar." Griff grunts in agreement.

"Besides," I continue as I approach Dair's body, "you know how Lucky is about following instructions to the letter. He told us to have a polite word with Mr. Dair, here. We did. He told us to offer him an out. We did. He told us to enjoy ourselves if he refused. I've got no complaints. Did you enjoy yourself?"

"I guess." Griff closes the switch-blade and puts it back in his overalls pocket. "He didn't play right, though. He coulda at least whimpered or somethin'."

"My point is," I roll the corpse over, grab the legs, and pull it into the yard. The white suit is covered in red stains now. A squirrel watches us from the other side of the yard chewing thoughtfully on an acorn. "Lucky didn't say nothing about bringing the woman with us." The face still has a smile on it, but it no longer gleams. I reach into my pocket, pull out two quarters, and place one on each eye, tails up. "All he said was not to harm her." I carefully fold the hands over the chest. "Small chance of that with the door barred against us." Finally, I straighten the legs and point the toes of the shoes up. The squirrel runs up the trunk of a nearby tree and disappears. "I'd say we're done here; wouldn't you?"

"Fine w'me." Griff walks across the grass to the van. "Let's go eat somethin'. I'm starved."

I feel positively giddy as I sit in the driver's seat and adjust the mirror. The sky is beginning to cloud over as Nan timidly opens the door and peeks outside. When she sees her husband spread out for the ravens, she runs into the yard with a scream, throwing herself over the body. She looks up at the van with tears streaming down her face and screams curses at us. As I crank the engine and pull away, I smile and wave, secure in the knowledge of a job well done and finally satisfied with my place in the world.

"You know, Griff," I say as I cut off a mini-van laden with yapping rug rats, "I've been thinking."

"Oh shit, we better get right with God." Griff punches the cigarette lighter, and I don't stop him this time.

"We need to get you a cell phone."

"What the fuck for?" Griff stares at me as if I've suddenly grown two snakes out of my head.

"I got it all planned: If there's some kind of nuclear attack or something," I slam on my breaks and swerve into the oncoming lane, "we could get in touch with each other at a moment's notice and head for the valley away from the fallout and ravaging hordes of radioactive mutants."

"Shut the fuck up and drive, Ziggy."

Challenge

Eighth grade
Early afternoon,
Body neither awake nor tired

Math class, algebra
Homework I hadn't done
Secretly scribbling
Answers as given
Can't have another zero

Across the room, a boy
Reads a book instead

Homework forgotten
I stare at the cover
All black and greys
A hint of red in the center

The sink of envy
As I watch.
He doesn't care about zeros
He does his own work,
Gets all the right answers
All the time
And the book.

Kid in the hall runs
"She blowed up!
They all dead!
Ever mother's son of'em!"

Homework forgotten,
We tumble to the hall
Teacher wipes her face,
Stumbles to assembly

I am last out.

That was years ago.
They say it was O-rings
Scattered astronauts,
Teachers, students to the wind

Today on my bookshelf
A book I've had
Since eighth grade.

Made in the USA
Charleston, SC
16 July 2015